My Story

PYRAMID OF SECRETS

Jim Eldridge

SCHOLASTIC

To Lynne, my continual inspiration

While the events described and some of the characters in this book may be based on actual historical events and real people, Nebka is a fictional character, created by the author, and his story is a work of fiction.

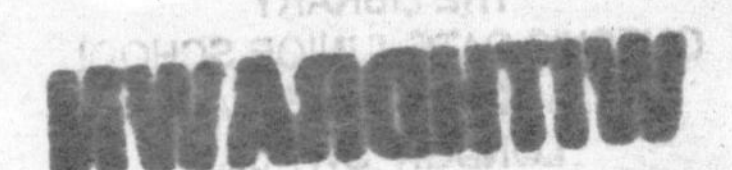

Scholastic Children's Books
Euston House, 24 Eversholt Street,
London, NW1 1DB, UK
A division of Scholastic Ltd
London ~ New York ~ Toronto ~ Sydney ~ Auckland
Mexico City ~ New Delhi ~ Hong Kong

Published in the UK by Scholastic Ltd, 2010

ISBN 978 1407 11656 3

Printed and bound by CPI Bookmarque Ltd, Croydon, Surrey

2 4 6 8 10 9 7 5 3 1

2517 BC

Egypt

Chapter one

My father died six years ago, when I was just six years old. The pyramid of Djedefre killed him.

My name is Nebka and I work for my Uncle Minkaf, my father's brother, in his fields and tending his goats. My uncle does not think of me as his labourer, he says that we are family and it is the duty of everyone in a family to work the land together. Uncle Minkaf says that all children have to learn the skills needed for them to work the land when they are grown. All I know is that other children don't seem to work as hard as I do, especially during the long days of summer, or to have such a miserable life at home. My uncle says that is how life is, that we have to work hard during all the hours of daylight to grow and bring in the food, and in summertime those hours are long.

My Aunt Ipwet is a hard woman, too. But then I suppos
that is because she comes from people that work the land, a
all landworkers are hard people. Except my father. My fat
was called Merire and he was gentle and kind. He played
me when he could, after he'd finished work. He used to
me with him to the fields and let me run around. Even thou

he had to work he found time to talk to me and take breaks with me.

Uncle Minkaf doesn't talk to me when we are in the fields, and there is certainly no time to do anything other than work. Play is not allowed. Uncle Minkaf says that being idle is a sin, because when you are not working you are not helping the household to build up its store of food.

It is true that my uncle's fields produce more food than my father's did, because my father wanted to spend time with me, and with my mother when she was alive.

I don't remember my mother much. She died when I was small, about three years old. She died giving birth to my brother. He died at the same time.

I think that is why my father chose to play with me rather than working the whole day. He said to me once that our time is very precious, and we should make sure we spend it doing what is important to us, to get the best of every day.

I miss my father more than I can say, especially when a day has been very hard and my uncle or my aunt have been particularly harsh with me. I wish that he had never died.

I said that the pyramid of Djedefre killed him. Well, he s working on building the pyramid, moving the big cut cks of stones into place, when one of the blocks fell and hed him. The big blocks of stone for the pyramid weigh tons.

was told that the wooden sledge on which the block was

being dragged collapsed as it was going up a ramp, and the block fell back down the slope on to my father. My uncle says he was killed instantly and did not suffer, but I overheard one of our neighbours who was working on that pyramid at the same time, tell someone that after the stone crushed my father it took him two days to die.

It is a tradition that when the great River Nile floods and the land is underwater, most of the farmers and field hands go and work as labourers on the pyramids, hauling the massive blocks from the quarry to the pyramid site under the direction of the engineers.

Then, about three months later, when the flood waters begin to go down, they leave the pyramid site and return to their fields. The soil is wet enough for them to sow their seeds and they cast them on to the wet ground as they walk. The waters of the Nile have also brought good things for the soil, which help the seeds grow and turn into wheat or other foods. Then, the following year, after the harvest the Nile begins to flood again, and the whole cycle starts again.

They are well rewarded for their work as labourers at the pyramids. The grain they bring back can help them through the hard times when the crops do not yield as much as they should.

I have never seen a pyramid, nor one being built. I have barely been anywhere except my father's land, and then my uncle's.

It had been a day when I had been spared work in the fields because my aunt needed me to work about the house, even though she complained all the time about how clumsy and useless I was. This time she wanted me to grind wheat and barley into flour so that she could bake bread. The wheat flour was for bread for us to eat, and the barley flour was to make bread that would be turned into beer for us to drink. Usually this work is done by girls, but my uncle and aunt have no children of their own, and so I am their son and daughter, doing all the work in the house and fields that they do not want to do. I often wish they had children of their own – then I wouldn't have to work so hard. Also, I wouldn't be so lonely. I long for the company of other children, but I only see them when people visit us. The problem is that my uncle discourages visitors. He believes they take up too much time – time that should be spent working.

As the daylight drew to a close, and I had finished the household chores, my uncle returned from the fields.

"I have been walking the fields and checking the irrigation channels," he informed us. "I met Ini, who was also walking his." Ini was our neighbour whose fields were next to ours. "Word has come from the officials that the Nile is preparing to flood. All the signs point to it. The Dog Star is in the right place in the sky. It is time for me to go and work on the new pyramid that is being built at Giza. And this time I shall take Nebka with me."

I looked at him, shocked.

"Me?" I said. "Go to the pyramids?"

He nodded.

"Yes," he said. "You are twelve years old. You are strong enough."

"Isn't it enough that I break my back for you here?" I retorted angrily. "You want to kill me off at the pyramid!"

My uncle scowled, strode over to me, and slapped me hard on the side of the head. It hurt and made my head ring. I stumbled back and trod on a platter, sending it spinning across the floor.

"You clumsy oaf!" roared my aunt.

"You will not talk to me that way!" snapped my uncle at me, ignoring my aunt. "I have fed you and given you shelter ever since we took you in. I have provided for you. I could have left you to fend for yourself, begging for scraps from strangers!"

I stood up and glared at him. My uncle was very strong. I would be no match for him if it came to a fight between us.

"You will come with me to Giza and you will work on the pyramid. You will not only learn useful skills, but also you will feel the glory of creating a pyramid for our king. There is no greater honour than that!"

"I will not work for the one who killed my father!" I shouted back at him. "I would rather die!"

"I've always said you've been too soft with him!"

spat my aunt. "He has become defiant! You should have whipped him more!"

My uncle stood still, glaring at me, and for a moment I thought he was going to hurl himself at me and beat me. But instead he just fixed me with his angry stare.

"Pack food for the journey," he said to my aunt. "The day after tomorrow, Nebka and I set out for Giza."

Chapter two

The next day my uncle and I worked long hours, walking the whole area of the farm to make sure the irrigation ditches were clear and the sluice gates between the fields were closed.

Every farm has irrigation ditches. These ditches come from channels that lead to the River Nile. At the time of the flood they bring the waters of the Nile right over the land and make sure that all the fields are flooded fully. Every field is surrounded by a bank of earth, low enough to make sure the flood waters can come over the top to fill the field and turn it into a lake. When the tide ebbs, the waters recede along the irrigation ditches to the Nile, but the low earth walls make sure water stays in the field. At the next flood, more water comes over the walls, making sure the fields are kept underwater.

Every field has at least one sluice gate in its wall. This is a hole filled with mud brick and stones and sealed with clay. When the time of the flood is nearly at an end, we travel around the flooded fields in a small boat and clear these holes. The waters escape through the sluice holes in the earth bank from the fields and flow into the irrigation ditches, back to the Nile.

When the fields are dry enough to walk on, my uncle and I till them with a plough pulled by an ox. This turns the earth over so that the good things the Nile has brought go into the ground and make it fertile, ready for the seeds to be scattered.

"Who will open the sluice gates and let the excess water out if we are both away working at the pyramids?" I asked.

"I have asked Ini to do it for me," answered my uncle.

As I have said, Ini's fields were next to ours. He had sons who worked his farm for him, and some of them were younger than me. Ini was too old to work at the new pyramid, so I guessed he and his youngest son would go around our fields and open the sluice gates, after he'd opened his own. If my uncle had already asked Ini to do this work, then it meant he had made up his mind some time ago that I was going to be working on the pyramids, but he hadn't talked to me about it, or asked me if I wanted to, he just ordered me to go.

Early the next morning, my uncle woke me.

"We have a long journey to Giza," he said. "The sooner we start the better. The boats will be sure to be crowded."

There were always boats going up and down the Nile, carrying goods and passengers, but at the time of the flood there were many more boats doing this journey, picking up the workers and taking them to the pyramid site.

My aunt had prepared our provisions for our journey: bags containing bread and beer. When my aunt saw us off she did not hug my uncle, just nodded at him. "Be careful," she said. "Make sure you come home safe." To me she simply said, "Stay out of trouble while you are there. Whatever you do will reflect on your uncle, and he has a good reputation to maintain."

It struck me that our sending-off would have been different if it had been my father saying goodbye. There would have been warm hugs and tears. Even though it had been six years since I last saw my father, and I had been just six years old at the time, I can still remember his arms around me and the smell of him, and his smile as he hugged me and said goodbye. That goodbye had also been at my uncle's house, because I was staying with my aunt while my father and my uncle went off to Giza to work.

I thought of that final goodbye as my uncle and I trudged along the dusty road towards the riverbank where we would catch the boat. In just a few days I would actually see the hateful pyramid where my father had died.

My uncle told me I ought to be proud to work on the pyramid. It was not only a monument to the great King Khafre. We would also be building two temples for him, his pathways to the Netherworld to ensure that he lived for ever. All our kings carry the soul of Horus, the falcon god. When they die, the tombs have to be built in such a way that the soul of Horus will pass on to the next king. The king who has died then returns to join the god Osiris, the father of Horus and ruler of the afterlife.

Although I heard my uncle's words about how wonderful it was going to be, all I could think of was that the pyramid had killed my father and taken him from me. I knew if I said this to my uncle he would get angry and hit me. My uncle believes the King is so important that we should all be happy to die for his greatness. I don't agree.

It was a four-mile walk to the place where we would pick up the boat, and we covered the first mile in silence. My uncle is not the most friendly of people and he considers "idle talk" – which means anything that isn't about work – to be a waste of time. Luckily for me, we met up with some other people heading for the Nile to pick up the boat. They were also on their way to Giza to work. Most of them were men and boys, but there were also quite a few families travelling together. The men and boys would be working hauling the blocks of stones to make the pyramid, and the women would be working preparing the meals and carrying out other duties at the site. I knew that in some cases, women also worked at the pyramids hauling the stones.

My uncle was happy to let me talk to some of the boys, while he walked along with the older men, all farmers, and they talked about the watering by the Nile, the problems of growing crops, animals, all the sorts of things that farmers always talk about.

Some of the boys were only a bit older than me, and two were going to work on the pyramid for the first time, just like I was. For one of the boys this was his second time of working on the pyramid. His name was Isesi, and he was fourteen.

"The great pyramid at Giza is so big you will see it long before we reach the site," he told us. "It is the biggest building there has ever been!"

"My father died building it," I said bitterly. "Six years ago."

Isesi looked at me in surprise.

"But the pyramid of Khufu was finished fourteen years ago," he said, with a puzzled frown.

I shook my head. "Not that pyramid," I said. "My father was killed while working on another pyramid: of Djedefre."

Isesi also shook his head.

"The pyramid of Djedefre isn't at Giza," he said. "It's at Abu Roash."

I looked at him, shocked.

"But my father worked on it!" I insisted.

"Yes," nodded Isesi. "If he was killed six years ago then he would have been working at Abu Roash. That's where the pyramid of Djedefre stands. The pyramid for Khafre we are going to build is at Giza, near to Khufu's pyramid."

A sudden burst of anger surged through me and I felt deceived by my uncle. He had not told me where my father had been killed. All I knew was that my father had died while working on the pyramid of Djedefre. I hadn't known the different kings had their tombs in different places in Egypt. I had assumed they would have them built together. I felt humiliated in front of these boys because I didn't even know where my father had died.

Isesi saw the hurt expression in my face and put his hand sympathetically on my shoulder.

"Don't worry," he said. "You'll be able to see Abu Roash from Giza. It's not far away and across a flat plain. You'll be able to see where your father died."

But he had misread my anger. Because my uncle refused to talk about things, I had appeared stupid in front of Isesi. And, what was worse, about the death of my own father, who I had loved so deeply. At that moment I hated my uncle, and the kings, more than ever.

Chapter three

We arrived at the landing stage where the boats would be pulling in. The Nile is the heart of Egypt, flowing from one end of our country to the other. It doesn't just bring life to the fields for food to grow and animals to be watered, it carries everything: people, livestock, stone from distant places for special building projects, all on boats made from papyrus. Because it was the time of the flood and so many hundreds of more people would be heading for the pyramid site, more boats were travelling than usual. We had been given markers so that we could travel in the special boats heading towards the pyramids at Giza. My uncle carried the markers for both of us.

The journey along the Nile was long. Throughout the journey the sun bore down on us on the boat, especially at midday when it was at its highest. There was some small shelter on the boat, but not much, and mainly for the sailing crew, so most of us kept our heads covered with scarves to try and get some shade.

After four days on the boat, we pulled into our final landing stage. The last part of our journey would be on foot.

Personally, I was glad to be back on dry land and feel the earth firm beneath my feet. The boat had rocked from side to side rather too much, and I had often felt sick, which meant I didn't feel much like eating.

Isesi told me the final part of the journey would take two days on foot, but it was flat terrain so it would be easy walking.

As Isesi had predicted, we saw the huge shape of the great pyramid of Khufu before we even reached Giza. The pointed peak appeared before us in the distance, shimmering in the broken light through a haze, when we were still a long way off.

The nearer we got to the Giza plateau, the more people joined us, all on their way to work on the pyramid. Nearly all of them were labourers or field hands; some with their families, others on their own. On the last day of our journey our numbers had swelled to many hundreds.

"And there will be hundreds ahead of us, and hundreds more following a few days behind us," Isesi told me. "Wait until you see the site itself. There will be thousands and thousands of men working. The first time I saw it I hadn't believed there were that many people in the world as at Giza."

I didn't reply. I had mixed feelings. On the one hand I felt the power of the pyramid pulling me towards it, as it pulled all these other hundreds of people; but at the same time the towering shape of the pyramid repulsed me because of what it stood for: death. Not the death of the King. That was ordained and the pyramid was indeed a sacred monument to preserve his body and spirit for ever. No, it was the death of the men who were drawn towards it, even as we were. Those who had died and those who were yet to die.

I mentioned this to Isesi as we lay beneath the stars on our last night in camp, before we reached Giza. Isesi smiled and shook his head.

"You are wrong, Nebka," he said. "The pyramid is not built for men to die. That is the last thing they want. The engineers and the King want workers to live, otherwise the pyramids won't be built. Fatal accidents are rare. Trust me, I know. I was here last year. Yes, maybe fifty men died, but that was all."

"And what about the year before?" I demanded. "And the year before that?"

"Even if it were the same number, it would be fifty men out of many thousands. More die in the waters of the Nile each year. And more die in the fields or from accidents."

What Isesi said was true, but it still didn't make me feel any better.

"The people who die in the Nile are usually fishermen catching fish to feed their families," I countered. "And those who die in the fields, die working to feed theirs."

"And the men who die building the pyramid die doing the greatest work of all, ensuring that the King will live on through eternity," said Isesi.

"You sound just like my uncle," I snorted. "That's what he says."

"And your uncle is right," said Isesi solemnly. "When I look back at my life my proudest thought will be that I did my part in building the temple of King Khafre to preserve him, and where he will be celebrated long after his death. People will look on this pyramid we have built and marvel at it. And I will know that I was one of those who built it in all its glory."

The next morning we were all up ready before the sun rose, and we prepared ourselves for the last stage of our journey. My uncle and I, and Isesi and some of the others, were at the head of the caravan, so we were among the first to see Giza up close.

I must admit, despite all that I have said about my feelings against Giza and the pyramids, the sight set out before me on the plateau stunned me and I felt an overwhelming sense of awe.

I had never seen anything so vast in my life. Not just Khufu's giant pyramid, and the site for Khafre's pyramid under construction, but the whole city. Because that was what it was before me: a city.

I had seen a town before, because now and then we travelled to the nearest towns for the markets. But the sight before me was truly staggering. There was street after street set with small houses and various other buildings. Some of the houses were like our own: small, made of mud. Others were long narrow buildings, set in rows. Still others, set apart from these long buildings, were huge and gleamed white from the limestone that covered them.

Beyond this city was a man-made lake, the largest I had ever seen. It was so much bigger than our fields during the flood season that it was more like a small sea. I could see that it had been man-made because the edges were dead straight and lined with roadways. There were sailing boats on it, which looked tiny from this distance, and made me realize just how wide the lake was.

Beyond this giant lake was the huge structure of Khufu's pyramid, with other smaller pyramids leading off it. And, beyond that, was the enormous base of Khafre's pyramid under construction.

And the people! Thousands of them! They moved around the site like ants, scuttling here and there, all busy working.

"Behold, the pyramids!" murmured Isesi.

Chapter four

"Come on! We don't have time to stand and gawp!" snapped a voice in my ear.

It was my uncle. He prodded me and ushered me forwards. I moved on but my heart was still thumping with the enormity of the sight before me. Had my father and uncle reacted this way when they first set eyes on Giza? I expect my uncle had just accepted it in his usual grumpy way and walked on towards the plateau, just thinking about the work to be done.

As we walked along the path on to the actual work site, Isesi nudged me.

"See those long buildings there?" he asked.

I nodded.

"Those are the barracks. That's where we'll be staying, The food was good here last year. Let's hope it's the same this time," he grinned. "The bigger houses are for the architects and engineers and other important people. Those really huge buildings in their own grounds over there, behind those walls," and he pointed in the direction of a large site near to the harbour, "those are the palaces for the King and his family and priests when they come to inspect the site."

As we walked across the plateau and got nearer the works I could see more of the area around the great pyramid of King Khufu, and realized it wasn't just one pyramid. The giant pyramid shone white and was surrounded by a high wall. Just outside the high wall, there were three smaller pyramids, with an even smaller one almost hidden behind them.

"What are those for?" I asked Isesi. "Those small pyramids?"

"Those are for the queens," answered Isesi. "Only one of them currently houses the body of a queen. Queen Meritetes, the mother of Khufu, is entombed there. The others are ready for Khufu's queens and they will be entombed in them when they die."

"And that very small pyramid?" I asked.

"That houses Khufu's *ka*. His spirit," said Isesi. "When his spirit leaves a king's body it needs a place to stay before it makes the journey to the stars."

I walked on, finding it all too much to take in. I hadn't realized the business of burying the King in a pyramid was so complicated. Despite his proclaimed love for the kings, and his years of working on the pyramids, my uncle had never said anything about this. Though it wouldn't have made much sense without my seeing the place for myself, so perhaps that was why he hadn't talked about it. Or perhaps it was just that my uncle didn't talk much about anything, except farming.

When we reached the small town made up of long barrack buildings, my uncle led the way to the overseer's office, with me, Isesi, and the hundred other people who had journeyed with us following him. There was a queue already standing outside and we joined the tail end of it.

By now the sun was quite high in the sky and people in the queue were seeking out whatever piece of shade they could find. Those who didn't want to lose their place in the queue, but found themselves in the glare of the sun, draped scarves over their heads and shoulders. This wasn't just protection against the heat of the sun, but also the flies that were everywhere. I was used to flies because they were a permanent fixture at my uncle's, hanging around the livestock and biting them, but here there seemed to be more than usual. Whether it was because of the thousands of people here, all attracting the flies with their sweat, I didn't know. All I knew was that there was a constant hum and buzz of flies hovering around and crawling all over us.

I thought of asking my uncle what we were queuing for, but he would only scowl at me and tell me to mind my own business. So, instead, I asked Isesi, who seemed to know everything, despite only having been at Giza the one season before.

"We'll be given our markers," he said. "From this we find out which barracks we'll be staying in, and which gang we'll be working with."

I looked at him, curious.

"What do you mean, gang?" I asked.

Isesi frowned and cast a quick look at my uncle, who was engaged in talking to another man just ahead of him in the queue. From what I could make out they were talking about crops and the flood season, so that would keep my uncle occupied.

"Hasn't your uncle told you how the system works here?" asked Isesi.

"No," I said. I nearly added, "He never tells me anything", but I thought he might hear, so I shut up and listened as Isesi explained things.

"The site has at least two or three thousand people working on it at any one time, mostly labourers hauling the big stones from the quarries to the pyramid. Some work here all the time, but most of the workers are seasonal. Like those of us who come from farms to work here during the flood. At times like this there could be four or five thousand men and about a thousand women working here.

"A gang is made up of 1,000 men, and that gang is divided into five groups of 200. Those groups are split up into ten smaller gangs of twenty men each. Twenty men together can pull a wooden sledge with a really large block of stone on it from the quarry to the pyramid, and up the ramps. Sometimes, if it's a smaller stone, ten men can pull it."

He grinned broadly. "With a bit of luck we'll both be on the same gang and then I'll have somebody I can tell off and boss around. We young 'uns always get bossed about by the older men, so it would be nice for me to have someone younger to pick on!" Then he laughed, to show he didn't really mean it. My uncle turned round when he heard Isesi laugh and gave him a glare, and for a moment I thought he was going to snap something out at him about this being no place for laughter, when the queue moved forward and I found myself being pushed forward towards the overseer's office.

"Stay there!" ordered my uncle, pointing towards the wall of the long building. "I'll register you."

"But I want to register myself," I protested.

"You're too young," said my uncle.

"If I'm old enough to work here then I'm old enough to register myself," I told him crossly.

My uncle glared and stepped towards me, and I flinched, thinking he was going to strike me. Instead, he stopped himself and pointed towards the wall. I sighed gloomily and walked to the wall to wait for him. Inside, I was angry with my uncle for treating me this way. First he told me I was old enough to go to work. Then he said I was too young to register. It was so unfair! I'd wanted to register myself to make sure I got on the same gang as Isesi. He was the first proper friend of my own age I'd made, and I knew that being in his company would help cheer me up as I sweated and strained to haul the huge stones for the pyramid.

Chapter five

I waited by the wall for what seemed like ages, watching men and women go to the overseer's table and receive a small piece of papyrus with an inscription on it. Isesi registered, and then came to join me.

"There's something different going on," he told me. "Your uncle has asked me to wait here with you."

"What for?" I asked.

Isesi shrugged.

"I don't know," he said. "But whatever it is, it's taking longer than usual."

Just then my uncle joined us. What was peculiar was that he looked happy. Not just ordinary happy, like when the crop had been harvested and gathered in. No, he looked so happy that his face and eyes seemed to shine in a way I'd never seen them before.

"I have been given a great honour," he said, and he could hardly contain his excitement. I felt he wanted to shout out loud with joy. But that wasn't my uncle's way. Instead, he whispered in proud tones, "I am to work on the Sphinx!"

This meant nothing to me. Was this a special sort of pyramid? I looked at him, puzzled.

"What's the Sphinx?" I asked.

My uncle looked at me, a hurt expression on his face as if I had insulted him. But then he realized that he had never told me anything about this Sphinx.

"The Sphinx is going to be a major statue to the glory of the King," he said. "It will stand to guard his pyramid. It will have the body of a lion and the head of a king. Nothing like this has ever been built before in Egypt! I have been chosen because the overseers know me as a man of honour and respect, and a hard and good worker." He put his hand on my shoulder. "One day, Nebka, it is my hope they will think the same of you and give you such an honour."

I could not see how this was an honour. It was still working as a labourer.

Then my uncle added, "Unfortunately, this means that I will not be working on the same gang as you. You will be on a pyramid gang. That is why I have asked Isesi here to join us. You and he are to be on the same gang." He turned to Isesi and asked, "I know you and your father to be good men. Will you take care of Nebka while he is here, and keep him on the path of goodness?"

Before Isesi could answer, I burst out, "But I am your nephew! I came with you! Why couldn't you get me on to the gang you're going to be with?"

To be honest, I was glad to be away from my uncle and to be working with Isesi, but I was so angry that my uncle could bring me all this way and then just discard me, like a worn-out shoe he had no further use for.

"Only the selected few may work on the Sphinx," said my uncle. "Perhaps next year, if you prove your worth and show yourself to be a good worker, I will ask the overseers if you can join me on the Sphinx, if I am given the honour of working on it again when we return."

"Of course we will look after Nebka," said Isesi. "I promise you he will come to no harm, and that he stays out of trouble."

"Good," said my uncle, and handed him something. To me, he said, "I will not be far away, but as we will be on separate sites, I doubt if we will see much of each other until it is time for us to return home. But, if you need me, Isesi will leave a message at the overseer's office and I will do what I can. Now, make sure you behave and make me and your aunt proud."

And with that he walked off.

"Come on," said Isesi. He thrust the small piece of papyrus from my uncle into my hand. It had a thin leather strap hanging from it. "Here. Hang this round your neck. The mark on it shows which gang you're with, and which is our barracks. So let's go there and get ourselves settled in."

Chapter six

The barracks where I would be sleeping was a long building with spaces for many men to lay their bedrolls. Most of the spaces had already been taken up, but Isesi's father, Huni, had saved two spaces for Isesi and me. As Isesi and I arrived another man, Pepi, was arguing with Huni, complaining about him taking this large amount of space for himself, but Pepi shut up when Isesi and I put our bedrolls down on the floor.

Part of me had thought it odd that my uncle asked Isesi to take care of me, rather than his father, Huni. But as I studied Huni I realized that he seemed distant in his gaze, and when I got close to him I realized he stank of beer. I then remembered how he had drunk a lot from his drinking skin bag on the journey, more than most, and how sometimes he seemed to be stumbling as he walked.

Beer is good for drinking, better than water because it is healthier and safer, but my uncle has always said that too much of it can harm you and make you do foolish things. Because of that the beer at our home is rationed, and often mixed with boiled water.

I used to think this was another example of my uncle's meanness: that rather than waste good beer he would water it down so that it would last longer. But, seeing Huni half-falling as he sat down too heavily on his mat on the floor, I realized that my uncle was right: too much beer of too strong a mix addled a man's brain and made him foolish and incapable.

"Are you all right, father?" asked Isesi as he went to his sitting father, concern in his voice.

"I'm just tired, that's all," said Huni. "It's been a long journey. I shall feel better after a night's sleep."

And with that he slipped down on to his mat, and within what seemed like just a few seconds, I heard him snoring loudly.

The other man, Pepi, scowled and spat.

"Huh, that's just what I need! Sleeping next to a drunk!" he snorted.

"My father is not a drunk!" snapped Isesi angrily at Pepi. "He has an illness and beer is the best cure for it!"

Pepi looked as if he was about to burst into laughter at this, but the angry expression on Isesi's face made him think better of it.

"Well, so long as he doesn't start doing odd things, I'm not bothered," said Pepi. "I'm a man who likes to be left alone."

With that he sat down on his mat and opened a leather bag, from which he took some flat bread and salted fish and began eating.

"We'd better get some sleep, too," Isesi said to me. "It's going to be a hard day tomorrow."

"And every day until we finish here," added Pepi gloomily, spitting out food as he spoke. "By the time you finish here, boy, the muscles of your back will be torn and your arms and legs will be shorter. But you'll be stronger. You'll be able to lift up a donkey with one arm, like I can." He looked at my thin frame with scorn, and then flexed his arms to show me the muscles of his biceps. They were indeed huge, and I was amazed someone that strong had backed down when Isesi challenged him. But then, power is not just in the body, it is also in the mind, and the fierce look of anger in Isesi's eyes when the man had called Isesi's father a drunk had been enough to warn off anyone.

Next morning we woke and I finished the bread we had brought with us for my breakfast, and then Isesi, Huni, Pepi and I set off with the men from our barracks to our assembly point.

I was going to work on the pyramid.

Chapter seven

My papyrus marker showed that my group of twenty men were part of a larger gang of 200, also known as a *phyle*, called "Green". There were five phyles in the larger gang of 1,000 men: "Great", "Asiatic", "Green", "Little" and "Last". The whole gang of 1,000 also had a team name. Our team was called "Friends of Djoser", the name of a great king from the past.

I had expected Huni still to be drunk and shuffling around, as he had been towards the end of our journey to Giza, but this morning he was wide awake. He still smelt a bit of stale beer, but there was nothing in the way he walked or talked to suggest there was anything wrong with him.

We walked to the overseer's office, where a man was waiting holding up a board painted with the same symbol that was on my papyrus marker: a pottery jug with a small stone next to it. When he had counted us and made sure that everyone was there, we followed him up towards the pyramid site. Already other men were at work, dragging wooden sledges with huge blocks on them towards the pyramid and up ramps. Though, at this time, it was just the start of a pyramid. A vast area of the limestone plateau had been quarried away to level it, with a low wall around it made of large blocks cut into square shapes. The first proper layers of blocks for the pyramid were in place.

"That first wall was the base of the pyramid," Isesi explained as we got near. "The engineers built low walls around the area and then flooded it with water, but only a very tiny amount so that it was only as deep as a finger length. Then they put down flat-cut paving stones until they reached the surface of the water. That's how they make sure that the base for the pyramid is level. Otherwise the pyramid will be unstable. It could even shift and collapse.

"After that, they keep putting the big blocks in place, like bricks in a wall, one layer on top of another."

I studied what had been built of the pyramid so far. Three layers of large blocks had been put into place on the base; each layer narrower than the one below. There was also a series of inner walls of large blocks. Isesi saw me looking at them.

"The inner walls are the tunnels and passageways inside the pyramid, which will lead to the tomb of Khafre, and where everything he needs in the afterlife will be stored," he explained. "In between the inner walls and the outer walls, the space will just be filled with rubble."

By now we had arrived at the pyramid, and the overseer called us to a halt beside a wooden sledge. He pointed at my gang, and told us this was our sledge, and that we should start work.

He then took the rest of the men to another sledge to assign them to it, and so on.

"Right," said Huni, grabbing up the long rope that was fixed to the sledge. "Let's go to work!"

We all took hold of the rope, ten on each side in front of the sledge, and set off. I didn't know where we were going, but Huni, who was at the front of my rope, with Pepi on the other one, obviously knew, because they headed straight along a flat stretch of road. Although the road was covered in sand, I felt the hardness of rock beneath my feet, and realized that it had been man-made. The road was just wide enough for two sledges to pass along it side by side.

With twenty men pulling, the sledge felt light and slid along easily, and soon we had covered the short distance to the quarry.

The quarry was huge. Basically, it was a hill of limestone from which blocks had been chiselled out, each as big as a man, and were now waiting to be collected and hauled away by the sledges.

I noticed that although some of the men working to cut these massive blocks of stone out of the wall of the quarry were dressed like the rest of us, in just a linen kilt and a loose scarf, they were roped together. Near these men were soldiers, armed with spears, who kept a close watch on them. I didn't have time to ask Isesi why these men were tied up because everything was happening very fast. We pulled our sledge to a halt beside an enormous limestone block, and Huni shouted at us to take hold of the long lengths of wood lying nearby. He had to shout to make himself heard because other gang leaders were shouting instructions at their crews, and there was the constant sound of hammers and chisels and sawing as the quarrymen and stone cutters worked the rock face.

I took a length of wood and followed the actions of Isesi and some of the others, sliding the ends of the pieces of wood beneath the block. Meanwhile, the rest of our team kept hold of the sledge to make sure it stayed in place right next to the chunk of rock. With Huni shouting out instructions, and calling for us to lift at the same time, we raised the side of the chunk of stone, and then levered it up so that it tipped on to the sledge.

The men holding the sledge held it firmly to make sure the sledge didn't tip over. Once the rock was on the sledge, Huni returned to the rope, the rest of us put the lengths of wood down and followed him. We grabbed hold of the rope and began to pull. At first, because of the weight of the block, it was hard, but Huni began to call out a rhythmic chant, "Tefnut, Ra, Khafre, Ra" and we pulled together to his rhythm like oarsmen in a boat. At each name he called out we threw ourselves forward with the rope, the sledge began to slide forwards faster and we made good speed to the pyramid.

A ramp of hardened mud and stones went up to the actual pyramid, and we hauled our block of stone up the ramp to where the stone masons and their labourers were waiting to push it into place. There, we used another set of long pieces of wood to lever the chunk of rock off the sledge, then we dragged our sledge back down the ramp to the quarry, where we picked up another huge block of stone, and brought that back to the pyramid.

We were just one of about a hundred sledges operating in this way, each one hauling the massive hunks of rock from the quarry to the pyramid. The whole site was a mass of non-stop sweat-driven back-breaking hard work.

Chapter eight

We worked solidly for ages, before Huni shouted that we could stop for a break. The sun was rising very high in the sky, and working in the middle of the day with the sun blazing down on you can be fatal. Even at home when we were in the fields, my uncle made sure we took a rest when the sun was at its highest, or else worked in shade. It's not just that the noon sun blisters your skin, it also dries you out. During our time hauling the blocks, women and boys carrying water containers had gone around every gang making sure that everyone had water to drink.

Everyone looked around for some shade to sit in. Huni and Pepi and most of the men found shade sitting beside some of the cut blocks of stone. Isesi and some of the others pushed our sledge on to its side and I joined them to use that for shelter against the sun. I was exhausted. My arms and legs ached and my back felt like it had been pulled out of shape and then brutally pushed back again.

"Hurt?" asked Isesi, grinning.

I nodded, too out of breath to actually speak.

"It's like that at first," he said. "But you'll get used to it after a day or two."

A day or two! I groaned to myself. In a day or two I would be dead from exhaustion, or my arms would have been pulled out of their sockets.

"Ah, here comes the food!" said Isesi brightly. Two women appeared carrying trays loaded with bread, and clay beakers, which they handed out.

"Bread now, dried fish later," said Isesi, biting hungrily into his piece of bread. "The fish is good, believe me."

I took my piece of bread and cup of watery beer, still aching in every part of my body.

One problem was that the smell of the beer, as well as the sweat on our skin, attracted the flies. They had been buzzing around us all day as we worked, but now we sat and ate they were all over us. I had to put my hand over my mouth as I drank and chewed to stop them from crawling inside my mouth!

I noticed that Huni only sipped at his beer, but that his hand was shaking slightly as he put the cup down. I thought this was strange because Huni had been so firm and strong as the leader of our team, driving us all on to haul the chunks of stone at speed. Isesi saw that I noticed this, and he lowered his head and muttered, "My father drinks too much beer. He knows that, so when he is working he does his hardest to make sure he doesn't drink too much during the day. Luckily, the beer here is watered down." He lifted his head and forced a smile. "I love my father very much, and he is a very strong man, but beer is his weakness and he knows it."

I decided to change the uncomfortable subject, so I asked, "Those men in the quarry – the ones roped together – who are they?"

"Criminals," said Isesi. "Most of the people working on the pyramids get a good reward for the work they do. But a massive job like this needs all the men it can get. So they bring convicted criminals here. Because they can't trust them to roam free like us, they have to keep them roped together in small groups so they can't run away, and keep them under close guard. And the best place to keep them in one place while they're working is in the quarries. At night they're kept in the Mastaba tombs." And he pointed towards the edge of the site in the distance.

"Are they dangerous?" I asked.

"Some are," nodded Isesi. "It depends what they have done to deserve being a prisoner. Some will have just done things like tried to cheat someone, but some have murdered. Those are the dangerous ones."

We sat and talked, and ate and drank until, after what seemed like hardly any time at all, a shout from Huni made us all look round. He stood up and drained his cup of beer. Isesi grinned.

"Time to go back to work," he said.

"But we have hardly had time to rest!" I protested.

"We've had long enough," said Isesi. "The sun is past its highest. And anyway, my father doesn't like to rest for too long.

He knows if he does he will be tempted to drink more beer. So he works. Which means those with him work as well. That's why the overseer likes my father to be a team leader."

"He's a slave-driver!" I grumbled.

"You'll get used to it," grinned Isesi.

For hour after hour we worked, hauling the huge blocks of stone from the quarry to the pyramid, with just one other short break in the middle of the afternoon. It struck me that field hands were the best people for this kind of work, because they were used to working hard and for long hours.

Finally we finished and returned to our barracks, but instead of going in I followed Isesi and the others to where food had been set out for us. An army of cooks was still hard at work, mostly women, cooking and baking and cutting up fruit and vegetables.

Beneath awnings of cloth and palm leaves to try and keep the dust and flies off the food, low benches were piled with things to eat. One bench was laden with bread. Next to that was another bench piled high with cooked fish, steam still rising from it. Behind the benches, fires burned. The fish lay on grilles, being turned by the cooks. Behind the table with bread, men and women worked together kneading dough and laying the flat unleavened bread on hot stones resting in the fires.

I followed the others in picking up a flat piece of bread

and pieces of the cooked fish. There were bowls of leeks, onions and garlic as well, which I added to the fish, using the flat piece of bread as a platter. Then I took a clay beaker of beer and followed Huni, Isesi and the rest of our gang to a space at one side of the town square. Everywhere was full of people eating and drinking.

I bit into the fish and bread and the vegetables and was surprised at how good they tasted. Much better than the food my aunt cooked for us at home. Or maybe it was because I was so hungry after having worked so hard and for so long, that it seemed particularly delicious.

"Good, eh, Nebka?" called Huni cheerfully, as he chewed on a piece of fish.

Now that the day's work was over he was relaxed and drank his beer with deep swallows rather than small sips.

"Very good!" I nodded, licking the flavour of the fish on my fingers.

"Fish, bread and beer!" continued Huni. "There is no food in the world as good! I would rather eat like this than eat the foods the King has to eat: duck and goose and beef."

"That is because you've never tasted them," countered Pepi. "If you were rich, your tastes would change."

"Never!" boomed Huni jovially. "This is the sort of food that keeps a man healthy. Bread for muscles, fish for the brain, garlic and onions to keep him healthy, and beer to make him happy."

"My father has a very simple way of looking at things," smiled Isesi. "But what he says has a lot of truth in it."

We continued eating until darkness began to descend, and then we headed for our barracks. I had intended to lay awake and think about all the things I'd seen today, at the strangeness of it all, but my body was so tired I fell asleep almost as soon as my head touched my mat.

Chapter nine

Next morning we went back to where the low benches had been set out for our breakfast. There was more bread, this time with dates and figs. Then our gang followed Huni to where the sledges had been left, collected ours, and once more began our day's work, dragging it to the quarries.

Even though this was only my second day, I was beginning to get into the rhythm of things. Our gang was now truly operating like a team of oarsmen in a boat, moving and hauling together at the same time. When we got stuck or slowed down, Huni would urge us on with the chants of the names of the gods, and we would pull to his rhythm. Although the work was hard, I felt proud that I was able to pull my weight with the rest of the team.

We were on our fourth run of the day, levering a block on to our sledge, when disaster struck. We tipped the block on to our sledge, and suddenly one of the wooden runners splintered and then broke under the weight.

"Curses!" yelled Huni angrily. "That is our sledge!"

I was puzzled at his anger, and Isesi started to explain to me, "Each team is responsible for its own sledge—"

Huni interrupted him, shouting, "Enough talking! Pepi, Nebka. You two stay here and guard our sledge. I don't want it being stolen and broken up for firewood – there are criminals here. The rest of you come with me and we'll get another while ours is being fixed."

With that, Huni and the rest of the gang hurried off, leaving me and Pepi standing by our sledge. Pepi looked at it, sunk and broken with the weight of the large block, and shrugged.

"No one's going to take that," he said. "If they do, call me. I'll just be over there."

With that he wandered off to talk to one of the guards in the quarries, who was obviously an acquaintance of his.

So I stayed beside our broken sledge. I had been standing there barely a minute, when I heard a harsh voice laugh mockingly behind me, "Well well! What have we here?"

I turned, and saw a tall man with a hideous scar running down his face from one eyebrow, across his nose and down to his chin. He was standing looking at me, and the scar made his smiling face something terrifying to see. He was roped to six other men. The sight of them was fearsome. Most of them had copper or wooden tools in their hands, and the way they held them they looked like weapons. Their hair was matted with filth and their bodies were covered in rock dust, which stuck to their skin where sweat had run down their torsos. They looked like demons.

"It looks like Ptah has brought us a present to play with!"

said the man with the scarred face, and the others laughed. Then they began to move towards me.

I should have called out to Pepi and the guard, but fear froze my tongue in my mouth. The answer was to run, but if I did that I would leave the sledge to the mercy of these convicts, and what would Huni say when he returned and found the sledge damaged further? By now the convicts had surrounded me, their iron tools held menacingly, mocking looks on their faces. I knew I would have to call out or I would be killed, but would I have time before they struck?

Suddenly an authoritative voice called out sharply, "Leave the boy alone!"

Another gang of convicts had appeared, another seven men roped together, and although these were also filthy and their bodies and faces covered in dust, there was something different about them. The convicts led by the prisoner with the scarred face looked like a pack of crazed animals. The new arrivals looked like men. Proper good men.

The man with the scarred face scowled and for a moment I thought he was going to challenge the newcomers, but then he grunted something and jerked his arm, and the gang of convicts shuffled off together.

The convict who had saved me approached, the others forced to come with him because of the ropes that tied them together. But this time I didn't feel fear.

"Thank you," I stammered.

"I am sorry if they frightened you," said the man. I was surprised at how gentle his voice sounded. He seemed more like an aristocrat than a worker, or indeed a convict. He smiled, and his smile through the dust and filth on his face seemed genuine and warm. "We are not all like that. We are not all criminals."

"But you are roped like criminals," I pointed out.

The man gave a bitter laugh.

"If we were criminals there might be a chance for us to be pardoned and released," he said. He gestured at his companions, who stood mutely studying me and listening to their leader. "Most of my companions you see here are political prisoners. Men who oppose the cruelty of the King. And, for that, they will spend the rest of their lives as slaves and be worn out and die." He sighed. "Me, I am different. I am the son of a king."

I stared at him, stunned, searching his face for a smile or a hint to show that he was making a joke. But his face was serious.

"My name is Ankhhaf and I am the son of King Khufu," he said. "You may not believe it to look at me, but I am the rightful king of Egypt."

It sounded incredible and, as he said, it was an unbelievable thing for him to say. But there was something in his voice, in his manner, in everything about him that made me believe him.

"Why are you here?" I asked, still stunned.

"Because I challenged the order of things," he said. "I do not think it right that the people of Egypt suffer and die to build such large tombs for their king. I said that a king must be of the people, not crush them into the ground to glorify himself, and that I would make sure that happened when I became king. But my brothers said I was dangerous and that I must not be allowed to make this happen. And so they had me captured and imprisoned, and stripped of all evidence that I was the true heir. And then they put me to work as a labourer, building the pyramid for my brother, Khafre." He gave a bitter laugh. "It was their way of making sure that I suffered every day at their power over me and over the people of Egypt."

I stared at him, still shocked by what he had told me. I looked at the faces of the men roped to him. Their faces were serious, and they nodded.

"It is true what Ankhhaf says," said one. "We were his guards at the royal palace and can swear to it. We knew Ankhhaf to be a true and honest man, who would put into practice what he promised. When Ankhhaf's brothers and their guards came for him, we tried to defend him, but they were too many. We expected to be killed, but his brother Djedefre thought it would be more amusing for Ankhhaf to spend the rest of his life tied to us and watch us suffer along with him. And when Djedefre died, Khafre made sure our punishment would continue."

"But … do many people know of this?" I asked.

Ankhhaf shook his head.

"The other convicts do," he said. "Which is why they obey me. The fact that I am born of the body of a king makes them wary of me. And the guards know, of course, because they are paid to make sure I never get the chance to escape. Because if I did, I would lead an uprising and take the throne that is mine by right!" And his eyes lit up with fire and excitement as he spoke. "I would ensure fairness for all the people of Egypt, not just the few! Not just the rich!" He looked scornfully towards the edge of the quarry, and to where the pyramid and the Sphinx were under construction. "There would be an end to this waste!" he said firmly. "No more pyramids!"

No more pyramids! The words went through me and filled me with excitement. It was as if Ankhhaf had put into words the thoughts that had been struggling to be heard within me, ever since I heard about the death of my father.

"What's going on here?" demanded a gruff voice. I turned. It was Huni and the rest of the gang, and with them they had another sledge. Huni glared at Ankhhaf and the other prisoners, and then turned to me. "Are they bothering you?" he demanded.

"No," I said quickly, shaking my head.

"Pepi!" called Huni.

At this Pepi appeared from behind some rocks, where he had obviously been resting, unaware of what had been going on.

"I told you to keep an eye on the sledge!" snapped Huni angrily.

"I was," blustered Pepi. "I only nipped behind the rocks for a moment. A man has to empty his bowels now and then."

It was a lie, and everyone there knew it was a lie, but Huni didn't want to waste time.

"Get that block on the new sledge, then fourteen of us will drag that to the pyramid, and the other six can drag the broken sledge along after us."

"Just fourteen of us!" protested Pepi.

"It's a small block," countered Huni. "And all of us will haul it up the slope to start." He pointed at me and five others, "You six will come back down and bring the broken sledge. Now hurry! There's work to be done!"

Chapter ten

That night, as I lay on my mat in the barracks, although I was as tired as I had been the night before, I couldn't sleep for the thoughts running around in my brain about Ankhhaf and the other men he had been roped to. Was it really possible that he was the true son of Khufu? That Ankhhaf should have been king, not Khafre?

I lay there, listening to the sounds of the night. In the distance dogs and jackals howled, and there were the noises of other livestock: donkeys braying, as they always did, cattle lowing. Nearer to me, Huni, Isesi and Pepi snored.

I thought about the secret I had been given. Or was it a secret? Did they know about it as well? If so, why hadn't they told me? Isesi was my friend, but he had said nothing about this.

It seemed so hugely improbable, but the other men with Ankhhaf had backed him up. They had been his guards at the royal palace, they said. And they did indeed have the manner of soldiers rather than common criminals.

I lay there and recalled the words Ankhhaf had said to me. Fairness for all the people of Egypt, not just the few! No more pyramids! If Ankhhaf had become king instead of Djedefre after the death of Khufu, my father would still be alive today! A sense of anguish and anger filled me at the thought. The cruel tyrant Djedefre had died peacefully surrounded by riches and luxury, while the true king was forced to labour in a quarry. And their brother, Khafre, had then taken to the throne and continued in the same way as his father and his brother; building a pyramid to glorify himself.

Yes, I know the pyramids were more than that. The pyramids were to help the king's spirit journey to the Netherworld and be reunited with the gods. But their tombs did not have to be so huge. The shape and direction of the pyramid were what gave it the power to keep the body of the king whole and safe. But a small pyramid could do that. These huge pyramids were just to please the king's vanity, and for that men like my father died. It was wrong! And it was even worse that the one who could change this and end this wrong, Ankhhaf, was kept a prisoner.

I must have finally slept, because I found myself being shaken awake by Isesi.

"Wake up, Nebka! It's time to get breakfast and get to work!" he said cheerfully.

I wanted to ask him about Ankhhaf, to find out if he also knew the secret, but something held me back. From the things he had said about the kings and the building of the pyramids, I knew that Isesi would not approve. But I had to talk to someone or I would burst!

I spent that day hard at work. Each time we went to the quarry to collect a block, I looked around for a sign of Ankhhaf, but he was nowhere to be seen. I wondered if he and his companions had been moved to another part of the quarry. Or, worse, had he been overheard talking to me by the guards? If so, maybe the guards had taken them away somewhere and silenced them. Killed them, to stop them saying those words again. But then I calmed down. The way that Ankhhaf had spoken openly showed me he was not frightened to talk about it. If he had said those things to me, a stranger, then he must have said it to others. And, as he said, the guards already knew the true story. No, it was more likely Ankhhaf and his companions had been moved to another part of the quarry. There were hundreds of men working in the huge quarry, cutting out stone blocks.

When we stopped for our midday break, Isesi and I sat down in our usual place leaning back against the sledge in the welcoming shade, with our bread and beer.

"You've been very quiet today," commented Isesi. "All this hard work taking your breath?"

I hesitated, wondering whether to say anything about Ankhhaf. It could be dangerous, and it could cause a rift between us, but I was so concerned I had to tell someone.

"Yesterday, while I was waiting for you to come back with the new sledge, I met someone in the quarry," I said. "He said his name is Ankhhaf."

At this, Isesi gave a broad grin.

"King Khufu's son," he laughed.

I looked at him, shocked.

"Yes," I said.

"I met him last year," he chuckled, obviously amused.

"But ... but why didn't you say anything?"

"What about?" shrugged Isesi, and he tore off a piece of bread and put it in his mouth.

"About Ankhhaf being King Khufu's son and the true heir to the throne," I said.

Isesi looked at me, puzzled.

"Why should I?" he said. "He's obviously either mad or he's lying." He shrugged. "Years spent working in the quarries can drive a man mad."

"But the men he was with said they had been his guards at the royal palace," I insisted. "They said he was telling the truth."

"Then they're lying as well," said Isesi.

"Why would they lie?" I demanded. "All of them?"

"Why not?" said Isesi. He looked around to make sure that there was no one to hear us, then he turned to me, his voice lowered almost to whisper. "Look, Nebka, you're very young."

"I'm only a couple of years younger than you," I protested.

"That's nothing to do with it," he said. "You haven't been out in the world like I have. You haven't seen the things I have."

"You've only been here one time before," I pointed out.

"You've spent nearly all your life on your uncle's farm. But I've met hundreds more people than you – all different kinds. Believe me, when I've been with my mother to take our food to market and helped her bargain the right price for it, it makes you realize how many liars and cheats there are out there. People lie and they exaggerate. Especially if they want something from you."

"I *have* met other people!" I protested. "I've met lots of people when we've had visitors, or been to town." That wasn't really true. As I'd said, my uncle didn't encourage visitors, and he didn't go anywhere much, except to talk to his neighbours who also worked their fields.

"That's not the same," insisted Isesi. "Those men in the quarry are criminals! They lie and cheat and can't be trusted."

"Just like kings," I said bitterly, "who want huge pyramids built to their glory and men to die building them. Like my father."

"Sssh!" snapped Isesi fiercely. He cast another look around to make sure no one had heard what I had just said. "That sort of talk is dangerous. You are insulting our king! You could be executed for that!"

"The *real* king would allow me to say out loud what I thought," I came back. "He cares for the people. He has been a slave and worked like a slave."

"That man is not a king!" snapped Isesi. "He is a criminal

who has either gone mad from working in the quarries, or is lying to make trouble. Stay away from him or *you'll* get into trouble." Then he added warningly, "If you want to stay alive, don't mention one word of this to anyone else. And don't talk of it again to me either."

Chapter eleven

During the next two days I carried on with work. I did catch a glimpse of Ankhhaf briefly, but at a distance. He was tied to the same men as before and was working, chiselling and hammering at the rock face and carving out great blocks of stone, but he was working in a different section to where our sledge was taking stones from. When I saw him my heart gave a leap. I wanted to go to him and find out more: about his life at the royal palace, and how his brothers had taken him prisoner, and how the rest of his family had reacted to that. I wanted to hear him tell me more about his dream for a fairer Egypt, where ordinary people could enjoy a life without being forced into this kind of labour. But I had no chance because Huni drove us on and we dragged our sledge backwards and forwards between the quarry and the pyramid. All the time the pyramid was getting slowly higher as the massive blocks were cut, dressed, hauled up the ramps and levered into place.

On the third evening after work I was sitting with Isesi, talking about the day and different incidents that had happened, eating our meal, when a shadow fell over me.

"Nebka," said my uncle's voice. "When you have finished your meal I would like to talk with you."

I felt a heaviness come down on my heart, and I shot a look at Isesi, wondering if Isesi had mentioned anything about me and Ankhhaf to my uncle, and my uncle was going to tell me off. But there was nothing in Isesi's face to hint that he knew what my uncle had come to see me about, and I had found Isesi to be honest. Also, as far as I knew, Isesi hadn't had any opportunity to seek my uncle out to talk to him about me, because our life had been solely: work, food, and sleep.

"I am just finishing, Uncle," I said; and I stuffed the last piece of bread into my mouth and stood up.

"This way," said my uncle, then he turned and walked off. I followed after him, wondering where we were going, and why.

We walked towards the pyramid that was under construction, and then turned on to the road. Then we continued along it and headed off along another path that went towards the place where the Sphinx was being carved out of a huge outcrop of limestone, and I realized that my uncle was going to show it to me. What puzzled me was, why?

When we reached the Sphinx he said, "Here!", his voice almost trembling with pride.

I stood there next to him, looking at the carving of a human head on a lion's body which was emerging from what had been a small limestone mountain left over from earlier quarrying. It was obvious that my uncle was really proud of what was happening at this particular place and wanted to show it off to me.

For my part, when I looked at the work of the Sphinx being created, I felt anger, the same anger I felt when I thought about the pyramids. The anger that it was these huge works that had killed my father. It was possible that the words of Ankhhaf had stoked that anger more, but that anger had been there even before I came to Giza. Listening to Ankhhaf, and realizing how different things could be, just made my fury that much more fierce.

"Behold the Sphinx!" announced my uncle, gesturing at the enormous carving under creation before us. "This is the first and the only one of its kind anywhere in the world!"

My uncle took me by the shoulder and led me to a board. On the board was a painting of a lion's body with the head of a king wearing a wide, royal headdress. I realized that this painting was to show what the figure would look like when the carving was completed. Now I had seen the painting I looked more carefully at the shape being carved and saw the outline of the front paws of the lion. About halfway along was what looked like another paw. I guessed there would be another paw on the other side. Near the back was what could be the tip of a lion's tail carved in the rock.

"What's it for?" I asked.

This was obviously not the reaction my uncle had been expecting. I guessed he had been hoping that I would be awed and proud for him. The happy expression on his face vanished and he scowled.

"It is the work of the King!" he snapped tersely. He turned back towards the giant structure, and his voice softened. "We have been told that this being will stand guard over the pyramid of Khafre and protect him. The head of a king and the body of a lion. The two greatest forces ever known, united here."

We stood there, looking at the foundations of what was to be. Once again I looked at the painting on the board. I felt I had to say something.

"It is very large," I said at last.

I had said the wrong thing. My uncle tensed beside me and glared at me.

"Is that all you can say?" he demanded angrily. "I am showing you one of the greatest wonders ever seen in Egypt, while it is still being carved. I am showing you the mystery of the gods as it unfolds. This is a sacred place, and this will be a sacred guardian of our king. I, your uncle, am one of those privileged men who will have helped this come to being. And all you can say is 'It is very large'!" He snorted and shook his head in disgust. "It is a waste of time and breath even talking to you!"

He looked up at the sky, which was darkening, and bringing night to the site.

"Come, we shall return to the town and sleep," he said curtly. "We both have much work to do again tomorrow."

With that he set off at a fast pace, back towards the barracks. I followed him. It struck me that this was the first time I had seen my uncle for days, and not once had he asked me how I was, or how I was coping with the work of hauling the great stones. All he wanted to do was show me this huge carving that was being done for the glory of the King, and tell me how proud he was to be a part of it. But all he was, was a builder. Not even that. He was a labourer. The King didn't care if he lived or died while he was building the Sphinx. My uncle was no more than a beast of burden, like a donkey. The same applied to me. That was all we were to this tyrant: animals to be used, and cast aside when our usefulness was over.

One day, I thought, there will be another king. One like Ankhhaf. One who cares. And he will be worthy of a statue extolling his greatness.

Chapter twelve

The next few days merged one into another, with the same routine each day: breakfast, work hauling blocks from the quarry to the pyramid, brief break for bread and beer, then more hauling blocks on our sledge until we finished for the day. Then food, mostly fish and bread but with different vegetables to go with them, and then a sleep of exhaustion.

Sometimes, after we had eaten and before we slept, I played a game of senet with Isesi. This is a game where two players move their pieces around a board using squares. The aim of the game is to get all your seven pieces off the board, while stopping the other player from getting their pieces off. Lots of men had brought their senet sets with them to entertain themselves in the evening. Huni had brought his, and he usually played with some of his friends, but now and then he let me and Isesi play. Isesi usually won because he had had more practice. We didn't have senet at home. My uncle would have frowned on it as being frivolous.

The good thing was that Isesi and I didn't touch on the subject of Ankhhaf, or the kings or the pyramids and so we talked again as friends. I told him about my life working for my uncle, and he told me of his life, working in the fields as I did, but also going to visit his different cousins, and spending time in the town with his parents.

It may have been the third or fourth day after Uncle Minkaf had shown me the Sphinx when our midday break was much longer than usual. This was because of Huni. I don't know whether it was because Pepi encouraged him to drink more beer, or because he felt he needed more beer, but the break stretched beyond the normal time. Isesi, who was sitting next to me, as usual, began to look uncomfortable as he looked across at his father, who was talking in a very relaxed way to Pepi. The two men were laughing together, but I felt that Pepi's laughter was not genuine. He was using talking to Huni as a way of delaying returning to work, and topping up Huni's clay beaker with more beer helped that delay.

Finally, Isesi got up and went over to his father.

"Father, we should get back to work," he said.

"Why?" demanded Pepi. "Your father and I are having a good conversation between friends."

"Because the overseer will notice and will make us work longer this afternoon to make up the time we have lost," said Isesi.

Huni nodded his head at this.

"My son is right," he told Pepi. "As he usually is." He pushed himself to get up, but then slipped and sat down heavily again. He shook his head. His eyes seemed bleary. "Old age," he muttered. "It becomes harder to get up when a man grows older."

"Let me give you a hand," said Isesi, and he held out his hand. Huni took it, and Isesi gripped his wrist firmly with his other hand and hauled Huni up. Huni stood and wobbled slightly, and Isesi moved quickly to steady him.

"Are you all right, father?" he asked, a tone of concern in his voice.

"Never better," Huni assured him. "There's no need to worry about me. I've done this work since before you were born." With that he turned and bawled at the rest of us, "Come on, you lazy things! There's work to be done! This pyramid won't get built with you lot sitting around!"

And he headed for the rope at the front of the sledge. I noticed that he stumbled slightly as he moved, but he recovered his balance and took hold of the rope. We all joined him, taking our positions.

"Right!" he said. "Onward!"

And so we set to work again. But I noticed that we didn't haul the sledge at the same speed as before. The pace was set by Huni, and he plodded rather than hurried. I saw a sly expression on Pepi's face that looked like a smile, and was sure he had engineered this deliberately by giving Huni more beer. Isesi was also aware that we were going slower, but there was nothing he could do about it. His father was the team leader and set the pace, and Isesi could not be seen to try and hurry his father along.

We hauled three large blocks from the quarry to the pyramid. Huni seemed to have realized that our rate of work had slowed down, because on our return journey with the empty sledge after the third block had been delivered, he picked up the pace, chanting the rhythm as before, "Tefnut, Ra, Khafre, Ra", but faster.

Pepi scowled when Huni began to chant to get us to work at this speedier rate, but Isesi smiled and leant against the rope to get the speed his father was calling for, as I did. However, I noticed that when we brought the sledge to a halt in the quarry, Huni stumbled slightly and seemed to be more out of breath than he usually was, and his eyes had a funny glaze to them.

While Huni, Isesi, Pepi and another man held the sledge firm, the rest of us picked up the wooden stakes and began to lever a huge block of stone on to our sledge, as we had done every time since we had begun. Huni was calling out the rhythm for us to push the wooden stakes beneath the block and lever it up a short distance at a time. Then, at one point, the balance of it would tip its weight over on to the sledge. I'm still not sure what went wrong because I was concentrating my strength and effort on raising the block, and then it began to roll as it passed the point of balance. As I relaxed from levering up and rested on my wooden stake, as did the others, out of the corner of my eye I saw Huni stumble on to the sledge into the path of the toppling block.

Quick as a flash, Isesi leapt forward and threw his father aside, but his effort made Isesi fall half on to the sledge, just as the massive block of stone came down, crushing him beneath it.

Chapter thirteen

For a split second everything stood still, as if the sun itself had ceased its journey across the sky. The bottom half of Isesi's body stuck out from beneath the huge block on the sledge, his legs limp. Huni stood and stared down at his son's legs, his mouth open and his face deathly white. And then he yelled, "Get it off him!"

Immediately we thrust our wooden stakes beneath the block on the sledge and began to lift it. This time we didn't need Huni to chant any rhythm, we all pushed feverishly and cursed aloud as we strained and lifted. As soon as the block of stone began to rise, Huni and Pepi grabbed Isesi's legs and dragged him out from beneath it. We carried on pushing and toppled the block back off the sledge, and then turned to look at Isesi.

He was dead. There was no doubt about that. His skull had been crushed, the bones of his head and shoulders smashed into pulp, his blood already being soaked up by the thirsty desert sand beneath him.

Huni dropped down beside Isesi's body and began to cry and howl. It was an awful sound, like a jackal suffering terrible torment. I looked down at Isesi's mangled upper body, and suddenly I felt everything in my stomach rush up, and I bent over and vomited. I vomited again, and again.

I sank down on to the ground, feeling weak.

Huni's howling brought others running, including an overseer, who stopped when he saw Isesi's dead body.

"You men!" barked the overseer. "Put the body on the sledge!"

He saw that we were all standing shocked and numbed, most of us, including me, too shocked to move.

"We must remove the body now!" he snapped. "Put it on the sledge and follow me." Pointing at Huni, he said to Pepi, "Take him to the overseers' hut and tell them what's happened. They'll deal with him."

Pepi went to Huni and tried to get him to get up, but Huni would not, or could not. He sat down on the ground beside Isesi's body and howled like an animal in pain, tears pouring down his face. It was only when we lifted Isesi's body and put it on the sledge that he stumbled to his feet.

"I must go with him!" he moaned, and he crawled on to the sledge and lifted Isesi's smashed body and cradled him in his arms.

Pepi gave the overseer a look of helplessness.

"Very well," grunted the overseer. "Bring them both."

We set off, hauling on the rope, dragging the sledge with the dead body of Isesi and his grieving father on it out of the quarry. The last thing I recall seeing were the convicts tied together, standing at a distance watching us, closely guarded by soldiers with spears. Among the convicts was Ankhhaf.

Chapter fourteen

We hauled the sledge to a part of the site I had never been to before. There, two men were waiting with a large sheet of linen. Someone had obviously run ahead to prepare them. These two men put Isesi's body on to the sheet and wrapped it up, and then carried it away to a low building made of mud brick. They did it so swiftly I guessed they were used to this sort of activity. The only problem was dealing with Huni. Huni wanted to go with them and the dead body of his son, but the overseer insisted that we held Huni back by force. Huni struggled at first, trying to fight us off so that he could follow his dead son, but finally he stopped struggling and sank to the ground, sobbing uncontrollably.

"You and you, take him back to his hut," said the overseer, pointing at two of our crew. "The rest of you, get back to work." Gesturing at Pepi, the overseer said, "For the time being, you will be the leader of this team."

Pepi bowed to him, and then barked at us to take the rope and haul the sledge back to the quarries. But this was only for show. I knew that once we were out of sight of the overseer, Pepi would slow us down.

I was numb with what had happened. My best friend, dead. The life crushed out of him because of one second of action: saving his father. I felt hollow inside.

For the rest of the day we continued to work, but it felt like we were dead men. None of us spoke. We just got on with our work. The whole time, as we hauled our sledge, I kept seeing the giant block falling on Isesi, and then Isesi's dead body lying on the sledge as we lifted the massive stone off him.

That night in our hut, Huni cried. No, not just cried: he moaned and howled.

I knew how he felt. My heart felt sick at the thought that Isesi was dead, that I would never see him again. Ours had been a short friendship, but a real one.

In between sobbing Huni moaned, "I killed him! I killed my son!"

Neither Pepi nor I said anything to him to assure him that wasn't so. For one thing, he wouldn't listen to us. And he had been at fault. If he hadn't got drunk at the midday break he wouldn't have stumbled when we were loading the block of stone on to the sledge, and Isesi wouldn't have died saving him.

I did my best to try and ignore Huni's moans and cries and try to sleep, but it was impossible. I couldn't sleep anyway, because every time I closed my eyes I saw the block topple and fall on Isesi. Pepi got angry the longer Huni's cries went on, and finally he got up and went out. He came back with an overseer and two other men, who packed up Huni's belongings and led him outside the hut.

"What's happened?" I asked Pepi.

"They're sending him away," he said. "He's no use now, and his wailing will just keep us all awake. Now go to sleep."

With that he lay down on his mat.

I lay back and stared into the darkness at the space where Isesi and his father had lain. They were gone, and I felt completely alone.

Chapter fifteen

The next day brought a change for everyone on the site. When Pepi and I reached the place where the benches were set out for breakfast, with the usual bread and fruit, there was a buzz of excitement.

"There's no work this morning!" one man said to us excitedly, as we reached the tables.

"What?" asked Pepi. "Why?"

I wondered if it might have anything to do with Isesi being killed, but instead the man said, "The King's coming!"

Immediately Pepi hurried off to talk to some friends of his, eager to find out more. I followed the man as we worked our way along the table, picking our breakfast fruits, and asked him, "What do you mean, the King's coming?"

"In a few hours the King, his family and his royal court will be coming here. The King wants to inspect the site and see how his pyramid and the Sphinx are progressing. He will be staying for a few days at the palace. We are to line the street along which he and his entourage will make their way to the royal palace and give homage. Then, once he and his people are in place, we return to work."

The King! Khafre himself! Despite my feelings of anger at the fact the pyramid we were building for Khafre had killed Isesi, as the pyramid built for his brother Djedefre had killed my father, I had to admit to a feeling of excitement and anticipation that I was actually going to see the King! My uncle, I knew, would be beside himself with pride and joy at the thought.

The man who had talked to me was obviously feeling equally delighted at the King's visit, but not because it would give him the chance to lay his eyes on the King, as would be the case with my uncle. "No work for the whole morning!" he said, smiling broadly as he bit into a fig. "A rest from pulling that accursed sledge!"

After we had finished our breakfast, we were gathered up in our teams by the overseers, and then into the larger gangs of 200 and marched towards the palace, which was at the opposite area of the site to the pyramid under construction and at the far side of the huge lake. This lake was linked to the great Nile by channels and canals – I'd seen the sailing boats arrive bringing grain and other supplies to the harbour along them. The King would be arriving the same way.

We continued marching until we were stopped by a wide road that led from the side of one of the man-made canals to the gates of the palace. We stood to attention by the side of the road, more than 2,000 of us, and waited. In the distance I could hear shouts as instructions and orders were passed from overseer to overseer, and I guessed that a series of lookouts was keeping watch along the river for the arrival of the King.

Suddenly the overseers barked commands at us to fall to our knees and bow down with our foreheads touching the ground in front of us, and I knew the King's barge was approaching. I knelt with the others. I was in the second row, which meant I was able to twist my neck and peer between the bodies of the two men in front of me in the first row, without anyone noticing that I was looking. I saw that other men were doing the same as me, twisting their heads to get a glimpse of the King. The overseers must have been aware that this was happening, but they chose to ignore it, rather than make a fuss and draw attention to us, and disrupt the King's procession.

The high prow of the barge appeared first, made of polished wood and decorated with gold shining out amidst the painted decorations of red and black. A mast towered above the barge, but at this moment the sails had been furled. Instead, I saw rows of oars on each side of the boat, dipping into the water and then out again in a regular rhythm.

The oars stopped and their blades were kept long enough in the water to act as a brake and slow the barge down. Then the barge was steered gently from the middle of the canal towards the side nearest to the gates of the royal palace.

As the barge was brought to rest alongside the wharf,

I realized that there were more barges following, all being rowed. They were all highly decorated, but none as grand or as beautiful as the King's barge.

After the first barge had been safely tied up, armed soldiers appeared from it and formed a line all the way from the barge to the entrance gates to the palace. They carried spears with them, and when they had reached their positions they stood to attention, the blades of their spears pointed upwards. I noticed that the blades shone in the sunlight, as if they had been polished, not like the spears carried by the guards in the quarries here.

When the soldiers were all in place men emerged from the barge, bare-chested and with bulging muscles. Between them they carried what looked like the base of a sledge, but it was painted gold, and had a covered tent-like shape on top of it with cloths hanging down to protect whoever was inside it from sight.

Then another followed, exactly the same, but painted in different colours.

Was one of them the King's? I wondered. But then a third such transport appeared, carried from the barge. This one was bigger than either of the first two, much more decorated, with much more gold painted on it, and with more men to carry it. This had to be the King's transport. The first two could be his wives, or other members of his family, or perhaps his Vizier.

Once these first three carriages had been carried along from the wharf, and in through the gates, the other barges began to disgorge their cargo: another carriage carried by strong men, also with cloths hanging down to protect the person inside; and then a double line of person after person, most of them dressed in all sorts of fine linen, many of them wearing elaborately decorated wigs. I had never seen such a show anywhere before. Finally, from one of the last barges, people appeared dressed in the plainest of clothes. These must be the servants, I thought.

When the last person had gone through the palace gates, the gates were shut.

Only then was the order given for us to stand.

As we were marched away back to the pyramid to start work, I looked towards the palace. The soldiers who had been part of the procession now took their place on guard beside the gates. More soldiers had taken up guard positions at all the other entrances into the royal grounds.

As I looked, I felt a surge of anger go through me. All that show, all that protection, for just a few moments' travel from the wharf to the palace gates. For this man, for Khafre, our king, men like Isesi and my father died. And I knew in my heart this was wrong. Surely, the gods did not decree this. Life had to be fairer than this.

Chapter sixteen

When we reached the base of the pyramid where our sledge was waiting, lined up with all the others, an overseer was standing with two men.

"These are Nekure and Sabni," the overseer told Pepi. "They are new to the work. They will bring your team up to strength."

Nekure was a tall wide man, built like a bull. He looked to be about 25 and very confident. Sabni was thinner and younger. In fact he looked like he was only a couple of years older than me, about the same age as Isesi. He also looked nervous about being here, as if he wasn't sure if he'd be up to the task.

Pepi looked at the two men, and then nodded dismissively.

"They'll do," he said. To the two men he said, "We're pulling a sledge. You don't have to be clever, just strong. Get hold of the rope with the others and just do the same as they do."

The two new men nodded and joined us as we went to the sledge. I picked up the rope, and found myself next to the younger man, Sabni.

"This is my first time away from home," he said. He

looked at me and smiled in a friendly way. "You're very young to be doing this kind of work," he added. I could tell that he was nervous by the way he seemed eager to talk. With what had happened with Isesi being killed, and because I still felt angry over the business of the King arriving, I didn't feel much like talking to him, or anyone.

"This work makes you grow old quickly," I grunted with a scowl. "Get used to it."

As soon as I'd said the words I regretted them, and my harsh tone of voice. The hurt expression on Sabni's face was as if I'd slapped him. He'd just been trying to be friendly because he was alone and nervous, and I'd sneered at him.

"I'm sorry," I apologized. "Things have been a bit difficult lately. I didn't mean to snap at you. And the work isn't bad, once you get used to it." I thought of what Isesi had told me, and added with a friendly smile, "The food's good."

"Stop talking!" barked Pepi. "Let's get this thing moving!"

And we set off, hauling the empty sledge behind us.

As we neared the quarry I could tell that something was badly wrong there. Usually there was a smooth flow of sledges: empty ones arriving, full ones leaving, with not much time between. Already there was a queue of empty sledges at the entrance to the quarries and none coming out. We let our sledge come to a stop.

"What's going on?" Pepi demanded of the team in front of us.

"Trouble in the quarry," replied the man nearest. "The guards have killed one of the prisoners."

A bolt of fear shot through me. Ankhhaf! It had to be Ankhhaf. He and his fellow convicts must have said something as soon as they realized the King, Ankhhaf's brother, was coming. I could imagine that developing into an argument, then a fight, and the guards striking him down.

"Shall I go and find out what's happened?" I asked Pepi. I was desperate to find out if the dead prisoner was Ankhhaf.

"It doesn't matter," shrugged Pepi. "It's a dead prisoner. It gives us another break from hauling this sledge."

"I can find out how long it's going to be before we start again," I suggested. "That way you'll know if it's going to be a long break or a short break."

Pepi thought it over, as I knew he would. If it was going to be a long break then he could go somewhere for a rest. I knew he'd hate the idea of just staying with the sledge if this disruption went on for a long time.

"All right," he nodded. "But be quick. And don't get caught up with anything. My team stays out of trouble!"

I nodded and hurried to the quarry, passing by the line of sledges and men. A few men grumbled as I pushed past them, demanding to know "Where are you going?" and "Who do you think you are?" All the time my heart was thumping as I wondered what I'd find when I got to the quarry.

What I found was an overseer talking with two of the guards.

On the floor at their feet lay the body of a man. I couldn't see his face, just the lower half of his body.

"It was an accident!" one of the guards was insisting. "He attacked me and I defended myself! And the other guards came to help me."

"That's right!" nodded the other guard. "We didn't mean to kill him. He fell on a spear."

A hand grabbed me roughly by the shoulder and spun me round, and I found myself staring into the scowling face of another guard.

"What do you want?" he demanded angrily.

"My … my team leader sent me to find out what was going on," I stammered.

"What's going on is that one of the prisoners attacked a guard," snapped the guard. He spat towards the dead body. "Luckily we killed the scum before he did any real damage."

So much for "falling on a spear" I thought bitterly.

Just then the overseer moved, and I saw the face of the dead man. It wasn't Ankhhaf. It wasn't even one of the other prisoners I had seen roped to him.

"My team leader wants to know how long it will be before we can load our sledge?" I asked.

"No time at all," said the guard, and he spat on the ground again, scowling at the dead body as he did so.

The overseer moved away from the two guards and headed out of the quarry, pushing past me as he did so. The guards in the quarry called a group of prisoners over and gestured at the dead body on the ground. The prisoners lifted it up, and shuffled off, carrying it away.

"Right!" the guard nearest me shouted towards the nearest sledge. "You can get back to work! Bring that first sledge!"

As the sledge moved, I stepped back, and then hurried along the line to where our sledge was waiting.

"Well?" demanded Pepi.

"Just a fight," I said. "They're moving the body now, so we can start working again."

Pepi scowled.

"Just our bad luck!" he snorted. He turned to the rest of our team as I took hold of my part of the rope. "OK! Get ready!"

"What happened?" Sabni asked me.

"A guard killed a prisoner," I told him.

"Ah" he said. Then he smiled. "At least it wasn't anyone important who died."

Chapter seventeen

At the end of the day, when we went to the tables for our evening meal, I saw that Sabni looked as exhausted as I had felt on my first day. He could barely walk, he was so tired. Even though I had only been working at the site for a few days myself, I was surprised at how quickly I'd got used to it.

The other new team member, Nekure, showed no signs of tiredness at all. He looked like a man who was used to hard work.

I showed Sabni the place where the food was laid out for us, and sat with him when we had collected our bread with fish and vegetables on it, just as Isesi had shown me on my first day. Once he had eaten a bit, Sabni recovered his strength and began to talk about himself and where he had come from.

"My father sent me because he has injured his leg so he can't work on the pyramids this year," he told me. "He says that someone has to come to earn grain for us, so he sent me."

"That sounds the same as my uncle," I told him. "He works on the land and he's always complaining there isn't enough for us and that I should work harder."

"Is your uncle back at home on his fields, like my father?" asked Sabni.

I shook my head.

"No," I said. "He's here, but working somewhere else. He's on the team carving the Sphinx."

At these words, Sabni's eyes opened wide.

"The Sphinx!" he echoed, awed.

I nodded, stuffing some more bread into my mouth.

Sabni shook his head in wonder.

"We have heard of the Sphinx in my village," he said. "They say it will be the most wonderful thing the world has ever seen. Even more wondrous than the pyramids!"

"It's just a huge piece of rock being carved into the shape of a lion," I shrugged. "Yes, it's big, but that's all."

"You have seen it?" asked Sabni, and his eyes looked at me with a new respect.

"Yes," I said. "My uncle took me to it to show me." I shrugged.

I didn't know what else to say to him. My uncle had been just as excited as Sabni over the Sphinx, and had expected me to be the same. Yes, the painting of the Sphinx I had seen looked strange and new, and the size of the foundations showed me that it was going to be truly enormous. Possibly even bigger than the pyramids.

But all I could see was the work that it would take to carve the huge statue, and the people who would die creating it.

People like my father, and Isesi. And the dead prisoner I'd seen in the quarry that afternoon. Sabni had said "At least it wasn't anyone important who died", and that's how we were seen. None of us who worked to build the pyramids and the Sphinx, or tilled the fields to produce food, were important. The kings didn't care about us. They pretended to, but all they wanted was glory for themselves, and they didn't care if we died so they could gain that glory.

"Do you want to see the Sphinx?" I asked Sabni suddenly. I felt I needed to change my mood and stop getting myself so worked up. Thinking about something else, walking somewhere, seemed as good a way to do it as possible.

Sabni looked at me with his mouth open.

"Are we allowed to?" he asked.

"I don't see why not," I shrugged. "My uncle took me to see it the other night. If he's allowed to, I don't see why I shouldn't be."

Chapter eighteen

It was growing dark as we reached the Sphinx, but it was still light enough for Sabni to be able to see the lion's paws and tail that were taking shape. He looked at the proud human-headed lion, and then at the painting of the Sphinx on the board.

"It is truly wonderful!" he breathed, his voice full of awe.

I looked at it with him, and saw it through his eyes. Up till now all I had seen was a shape being carved out of a small hill of limestone. Perhaps it was because my uncle was so proud of the Sphinx and his part in carving it, and I felt such anger at him that I refused to see the Sphinx as anything special. Now, even I had to admit that this Sphinx was something magnificent.

As I looked at the Sphinx I thought again of Ankhhaf, at this time of night imprisoned in the Mastaba tombs along with the other prisoners. I wanted to talk to him and hear more of his story. I wanted to hear more of his dreams for change.

"Sabni," I said. "I have to go and check on something."

"What?" he asked.

I hesitated. I didn't want to tell him about Ankhhaf in case he blurted it out and got me into trouble. "It's something over at the Mastaba tombs," I said.

Sabni looked frightened.

"You shouldn't go anywhere near them!" he said. "That's where they keep the convicts at night!"

"I know," I told him. "It's nothing dangerous. I just need to check on something. You don't have to come with me."

"I won't!" he said fervently. "And you shouldn't go there either!"

"I'll be all right," I assured him. "You go back to the barracks. I'll see you there."

With that, I headed towards the edge of the site where the Mastaba tombs were. These tombs were still under construction, and would be where important people would be buried one day, such as scribes and priests. When the tombs were finally finished they would have proper flat-roofed buildings erected over them; but at the moment they were just deep shafts in the ground that led to where the actual tombs were being dug. At night the prisoners were untied and then sent down ladders into the shafts where they took protection against the weather by sheltering in the half-dug tombs. Once the prisoners were down the shafts, the ladders were pulled up until the morning.

As I approached the tombs, I was surprised to see a small group of men sitting together near the edge of one of the deep shafts. Two guards armed with spears were sitting crouched some distance away from them, and as I drew near one of the guards got up and came towards me, his spear levelled pointing at me.

"Stop!" he ordered.

I stopped, wondering what was going on. I had expected all the prisoners to be in the shafts. My plan had been to get to the edge and look down, just to see them, and see if I could talk to Ankhhaf. I hadn't expected the guards to be so close by, or for any of the prisoners to be above ground.

"What are you doing here?" demanded the guard.

"I … I just came for a walk," I said. "I am a worker here."

"It is the boy!" said a voice I recognized as Ankhhaf's, and as I watched one of the group of prisoners stood up. Although he was still roped to the others, it was definitely Ankhhaf.

"Let him come through!" he called. "He means no harm."

The guard hesitated, then scowled.

"I already do you too many favours," he growled. "All right, you can have a few words with him, then it's time for you to go down the shaft. I need my rest."

"I am grateful," said Ankhhaf. "You will be rewarded, I promise."

"And sooner rather than later, I hope," muttered the guard.

He lowered his spear, and I hurried to where Ankhhaf and the other prisoners were sitting. I saw that they were the same group of men I had met with Ankhhaf previously.

"Welcome," said Ankhhaf. He smiled and gestured for me to join them. "You will be safe with us, I promise you."

I sat down on the sand next to them. The other men seemed nervous with me being there, but my arrival seemed to have a relaxing effect on Ankhhaf.

"How is it that you are sitting here, instead of down in the tombs?" I asked.

"We bribe the guards with our food ration to be allowed to sit near the entrance for an hour or two on some evenings," explained Ankhhaf. "Just to see something other than the rock walls of the quarry and the tombs below. It may be only a small thing, but for men like us, it reminds us that once upon a time we were free men."

Suddenly, one of the other men burst out, "Ask him before the guard comes!"

"Peace, Mekhu," said Ankhhaf to the man. "Let the boy settle first and get to know us."

"Ask me what?" I asked, puzzled.

Ankhhaf hesitated, then nodded. His smile had gone and been replaced by a serious expression.

"Mekhu is right," he sighed. "There is no time. At any moment the guards may come over and put us down into the tombs."

"Ask me what?" I repeated, more firmly this time.

Ankhhaf looked intently into my face.

"Did you believe what we told you last time?" he asked. "About who I really am, and who my companions are?"

"Yes," I nodded.

"And do you remember what I said I would do if I were king?"

"No more pyramids," I said, nodding.

"No more pyramids," he echoed, also nodding. "Fairness for all the people of Egypt." Then he gave a smile, but this one bitter. "I understand my brother arrived today."

"King Khafre," I nodded.

"Was his entry magnificent?" asked Ankhhaf. "Was he surrounded by riches?"

"Yes," I said.

"Ask him!" said Mekhu again, his tone even more urgent.

Ankhhaf ignored him, but looked directly into my eyes. Even in the half-light of dusk I could see his eyes, see the honesty and truth in them.

"What is your name, boy?" he asked.

"Nebka," I told him.

"Nebka, I need to see my brother," said Ankhhaf. "I need to talk to him. If I can talk to him I am sure I can persuade him to reinstate me. When we were children together, Khafre was the one I was closest to. He was the one who didn't want to have me imprisoned. He loved me, but he was overruled by Djedefre and the others."

"Then why doesn't he free you?" I asked.

"Because he will have been told that I am dead." Ankhhaf gestured at the shafts that led down to the tombs. "Not many men survive long in these places."

"But how can you talk to him?" I asked. "I am sure he will not be coming to the quarry, and certainly not to these tombs. And even if he does, surely they will keep you well away from him."

"Exactly so!" nodded Ankhhaf. He turned to the others, smiling. "See, the boy understands!" Turning back to me, he said, "There is only one way for me to see my brother and talk to him. That is for me and my companions to get out of the tombs at night and go to the palace. I will send him a message telling him I am alive. I know he will see me."

"The guards will not let you in," I said.

"Yes they will," Ankhhaf insisted. "There are still those amongst the guards who will remember me."

"And who will remember us, their comrades," added another of the men.

"But we can only do that if we can get to the palace," said Ankhhaf. "Will you help us?"

I looked at them, from one to another, bewildered. What could I, a twelve-year-old boy, do that these men could not?

Ankhhaf saw from my expression my puzzlement, and answered it, even though I had not put it into words.

"We are tied up and guarded closely during the day. The only time we are not tied up is at night when we are down below in the tombs." He lowered his voice and gestured to where the ladders were lying. "If you could manage to push one of those ladders down into the shaft at night, we could climb up and escape."

I looked at him doubtfully.

"But there are guards," I pointed out.

"At night there are only two guards at any one time," replied Ankhhaf. "The shafts are deep and we cannot climb the sheer walls, so they don't expect us to even try and get out. And some of the guards are more lax than others. Tonight's guards are strict, although they can be bribed. But in two nights' time two particularly lazy guards will be on duty. We believe they spend most of their time asleep."

I thought it over. Helping prisoners escape! The thought of it sent shivers down my spine.

"I don't know…" I began doubtfully.

"I told you he would not help us!" snapped Mekhu angrily. "He is like all the rest! He says all the right things and talks sympathetically but he does nothing to help make Egypt a fairer place!"

"No, Mekhu!" Ankhhaf said to Mekhu. "Nebka is right to have doubts. After all, we could be lying to him about who I am."

"No," I said. "No, I know you are not lying!"

"Then help us," Ankhhaf appealed to me. "Help the people of Egypt."

As I looked at him, at the honesty in his eyes and the sincerity in his voice, I knew that I really was his only chance. And not just his chance, but the chance to overthrow the tyrants and bring fairness to all Egyptians. No more pyramids!

"Yes," I whispered, nodding. "I will help you."

Just then we heard a sharp voice yell, "Right, time's up!"

We turned and saw the two guards approaching us. They were carrying a long wooden ladder, which they lowered down one of the shafts. Then, while one of them stood guard with his spear held ready for use, the other called Ankhhaf and his comrades over.

"Come on, hurry up!" called the guard. "Before the changeover guards get here, otherwise they'll want a share of your rations, too."

The men got to their feet. Ankhhaf turned to me.

"You will come to us in two nights' time?" he whispered urgently.

"I will!" I promised him.

Then the men headed for the ladder which would take them down into the shaft.

I turned and headed back towards the barracks. As I did, I met two men with spears walking towards the tombs. These must be the next watch, I thought, about to take over from the other guards.

"You!" called one of the new arrivals. "What are you doing here?"

"I ... I was just out for a stroll," I said.

"Let's see your mark," growled the guard suspiciously.

I held up my papyrus to show it to him. As I did so, the other guard said, "I know you! You're that nephew of Minkaf's."

"Yes," I said.

The first guard scowled.

"If you're a nephew of Minkaf's I'm surprised he let you come out to the tombs," he said. "The men here are dangerous."

"My uncle doesn't know I'm here," I said. "I didn't come here on purpose. I was just walking."

"Well don't come walking here again," snapped the guard.

"Yes, sir," I nodded, and I hurried off.

The two guards continued on their way towards the tombs, to change over.

As I hurried back to the barracks, such a feeling of excitement filled my whole body that I wanted to burst. I was going to bring fairness to all the people of Egypt!

Chapter nineteen

When I got back to my barracks, Pepi was sitting outside the door waiting for me.

"Where have you been?" he demanded.

"Out for a walk," I replied.

"I hear you went for more than just a walk," said Pepi. "I hear you went over to the tombs where the prisoners are."

I saw Sabni standing just inside the door. I could tell by the way he stood, very nervous, and the unhappy look on his face that he had told Pepi where I'd gone.

"So?" I demanded. "I'm a free person."

Pepi glared at me, then suddenly swung his hand and hit me on the side of the head, just as my uncle had struck me.

"No, you're not!" he snapped at me. "You're on my team. You do what I say. From now on you don't go near those tombs. Understand?"

I glared at him. My ears were still ringing and my face stung where he had hit me.

Pepi scowled and thrust his face nearer to mine.

"I won't have a kid disobey me. I asked if you understood."

As I looked at him I felt a great feeling of anger rise up in me.

I wanted to punch him, but I knew if I did he'd beat me to the ground and hurt me very badly. I swallowed and nodded.

"I understand," I said.

"Good," he said. He jerked his head at the doorway to the barracks. "Now get in there and get some sleep."

I went in. My fists were clenched so hard with my rage against Pepi that they ached.

"I'm sorry," apologized Sabni. "He asked me where you were. I didn't know it was forbidden."

I looked around to see if Pepi could hear me, and saw that he was sitting outside, just out of earshot.

"It's not forbidden," I muttered. "It's just Pepi showing that he's in charge. He only did it because I'm young. He wouldn't have done it to Nekure if he had gone to the tombs."

I looked around.

"Where is Nekure?" I asked.

"I saw him outside, talking to some other men," said Sabni.

"He'll come back drunk," I said. "He looks the type. With a bit of luck he'll punch Pepi and damage him."

I went to my mat and lay down on it. Sabni followed me and stood by me, nervous.

"I really am sorry," he apologized. "I didn't know what to do when I got back. I felt all alone. I've never been away from home before."

"Yes, I know, you told me," I grunted unsympathetically.

At that moment I just felt angry at him. It was because of him I'd been struck hard around the face by Pepi.

I turned my back on him, but I was aware that he was still standing there, hovering.

"What happened?" he asked, his voice an excited whisper.

"When?" I asked.

"At the tombs? Did you see the prisoners?"

"Nothing happened," I said. "A guard told me to go away. That was it. Nothing happened."

Sabni still didn't move from behind my mat. There was a pause, then he said, "I was worried because you might have been in danger. That's why I told Pepi where you were. You're the only person here who's been nice to me."

I listened to the tremble in his voice, and realized that he was telling the truth. I rolled over, and saw that he was crouched down beside my mat. The unhappy expression on his face was so deep it looked as if he might burst into tears.

"OK," I nodded. "I'm sorry I was harsh just now. That slap from Pepi hurt."

"I know," he said, looking even more miserable. "It was my fault."

"Don't worry about it," I told him. "I've been hit harder than that before, and I'm sure I will be again. Just go to sleep."

Sabni's face brightened up at that.

"Then, we are still friends?" he asked.

"Yes," I nodded. "We are still friends."

He smiled.

"Thank you," he said. "I don't know if I could survive this place without a friend."

With that, he went to his mat and lay down.

I thought about his words, and what it must be like for Ankhhaf. How many years had he spent chained as a convict, working in the quarries? Day after back-breaking day, roped to the others like an animal; and then kept in the deep shaft of the tombs at night.

I could scarcely sleep that night because of the feeling of nervousness over what I was going to do in just two nights' time. I was going to sneak to the tombs and push a ladder down one of the shafts and help Ankhhaf and his comrades escape.

I started to panic as I thought about what would happen to me if I was caught. Already the guard at the tombs had warned me off going back there at night, as had Pepi. If I was caught then the least that would happen to me would be that I would be sent away from Giza. And if that happened there was no way I could go back to my aunt and uncle's. I would become a wanderer, alone. I would end up as a beggar on the streets of the town.

At worst, I would be found guilty of trying to help convicts and would be sent to the quarries myself as a prisoner, roped up with them for the rest of my life. I'd be beaten by the guards, and by the harsher prisoners: the real murderous criminals who were there.

These thoughts terrified me so much that I couldn't sleep. I lay on my mat and listened to Sabni and Pepi breathing easily as they slept, and envied them.

Nekure came in, and although he stank of beer he didn't make any more noise than usual. He just lay down on his mat and was asleep within seconds, snoring loudly.

I lay and saw visions of myself tied to the other prisoners in the quarries and being beaten by guards, or being beaten and arrested by soldiers for begging in the town.

"I can't go through with it," I whispered to myself. "I shall tell Ankhhaf I can't do it."

But then I remembered the sight of Isesi's dead body, his head smashed, and my father, killed by a huge block of stone, and all the others who would die as the building went on, and the riches of the King's procession to the palace. Then in my mind I heard Ankhhaf's voice say "No more pyramids!", and I knew I would do it. I would push the ladder down the shaft and release Ankhhaf, and bring fairness to the people of Egypt.

Chapter twenty

I did sleep, but for how long I don't know. It seemed to me I had just a few moments before Pepi was shaking me awake.

"Come on, boy!" he snapped. "There's work to be done."

That day was painful for me. Because of the lack of sleep, every haul of the sledge was misery and ached throughout my body. My arms and legs and shoulders cried out with pain. I was grateful for every break we took. Fortunately for me, Pepi was happy to extend each break for as long as he could, unlike Huni, who had kept the breaks short so that we could work more.

By the time the end of the day came I felt like I would have to crawl to the benches for the meal set out for us. Sabni noticed I was struggling as we walked along.

"Are you ill?" he asked.

"No, just tired," I said. "I didn't sleep much last night."

"Was that because of what Pepi did to you?" he asked. "Hitting you like he did?"

I nodded.

"Yes," I said. "My anger kept me awake."

It was easier than telling him the truth. Especially as I

knew he would try and talk me out of it or, even worse, he would tell someone else what I was planning, in order to stop me.

Sabni and I were eating our meal when I saw my uncle walking towards us. He stopped beside me. His face looked serious.

"Nebka," he said, "I need to talk to you."

I gestured at the piece of bread and fish I was holding.

"I'm eating," I told him. "Can we talk later?"

The truth was, I didn't want to talk to him at all. Every time he wanted to talk to me, it was just to tell me off about something. My guess was that the guard at the tombs had told him about my going there the night before. He had said he recognized me as "Minkaf's nephew". My uncle had been coming to the pyramid site for years to work during the time of the flood, and he would know lots of the other workers.

"I need to talk to you now," said my uncle firmly. He turned to Sabni and said, "Go. I must talk to my nephew in private."

His tone was so fierce that Sabni immediately got up and walked away, and sat somewhere else. My uncle sat down where Sabni had been sitting.

"I've been told you went to the tombs last night," my uncle said.

My heart sank. I knew it!

"Yes," I said. "I was just taking a walk in the evening air."

My uncle glared at me.

"Don't lie," he snapped. "You were talking to the prisoners. I heard it from the guards."

"I'm not lying," I said. "I went for a walk near to the tombs and when I got there I found some prisoners there."

"And you talked to them," said my uncle accusingly.

"Yes," I said. "What's wrong with that?"

"Those men are criminals!" thundered my uncle. "Thieves and robbers and murderers!"

"Not all of them," I countered.

"You are a fool!" thundered my uncle. "Do you think they are kept tied up and under close guard because of how good they are? Every one of those men is dangerous."

I was about to snap back at him that not all of them were and tell him about Ankhhaf, but then I thought better of it. It would just make him even angrier.

"I have been working here for years," he continued. "The overseers and the guards and many of the other workers know me as an honest, hard worker. My good name is the most important thing I have. I will not have that ruined by the stupid actions of my useless nephew."

"I am not useless!" I snapped back angrily. "I work as hard as any man on my team. Ask anyone! Ask Pepi! Ask the overseers, who will have watched me work."

My uncle fell silent at this, and then he nodded reluctantly.

"It is true you have worked well since you have been here," he admitted. "I have talked to the overseers and they say good things about you. You are not lazy. Unlike some of the men on your team." He showed an expression of disgust as he said that, and I guessed he was talking about Pepi, but didn't like to say his name. Then his face grew grim again. "That is why it is even more important that you behave well. If you do, you can return here again next year, and every year after. There will always be work for good strong men, work that is well rewarded." He looked me squarely in the eye. "So listen to me, Nebka, and listen well. You will behave. You will not go to the tombs again. You will not talk to the prisoners. If you do, I will make sure you are sent home and your Aunt Ipwet will take a firm hand with you there. Do you understand me?"

I hesitated.

"I said, do you understand me?" demanded my uncle, his voice low with threat.

"Yes," I said. "Yes, I understand you."

"Good," he said. "Because I will be watching you. And I will ask those who know me to watch you. You have been warned, Nebka."

With that, Uncle Minkaf got up and strode away. I sat and watched him go. Inside me there was a mixture of anger at him for the way he had spoken to me, and fear because I knew what he threatened was true: he would be watching me, or have his cronies watch me. How could I get to the tombs tomorrow night and push the ladder down the shaft without my uncle finding out?

Chapter twenty-one

I spent the next day hauling the sledge with the rest of my team, and thinking about getting the ladder down the tomb shaft that night. Worrying about this affected me throughout the day. When Sabni and I sat down to eat our midday meal, Sabni said to me, "You are very quiet today, Nebka. Are you still worried about what happened yesterday? First Pepi, and then your uncle threatening you about you going to the tombs?"

I shook my head.

"No," I lied. "I didn't sleep well last night, so I'm feeling tired today. I'll be all right later."

"But you didn't sleep well the night before, either," said Sabni, concerned. "If you don't sleep properly you won't be fit for work and you'll get ill."

I forced a reassuring smile for Sabni's benefit.

"Don't worry," I said. "I'll sleep well tonight. Then tomorrow I'll be fine."

Sabni seemed satisfied by my explanation, but beneath my smile and my casual manner, I was starting to feel a rising sense of panic. I did my best to push what I had promised to do to the back of my mind, but it was always there, haunting me, as we toiled and laboured hauling the blocks of stone.

That evening after work, I ate my meal with Sabni and we talked about many things. Or, rather, Sabni talked and I listened. He talked about his life at home and his two sisters, both younger than him, and how already they were thinking about the men they were going to marry.

"My father says I should get married as well," said Sabni. "He says if I leave it too late then all the best girls will be taken." He laughed. "He and I have different views of what sort of wife would do for me. The girl I have my eye on is really beautiful, but my father says that a poor man needs a wife who is strong. Beauty is for the rich, he says."

I listened to him talk about his life and his dreams for the future, and couldn't help but think that my own future might be very short indeed. If I was caught helping Ankhhaf and the other prisoners get free, then any chance of a happy future would be at an end. My life from this evening would be spent as a convict.

But then I thought of how Isesi and my father had died, and the promise that Ankhhaf had made to me. No more pyramids! No more deaths!

When I thought of that, I knew I had no choice.

After our meal Sabni and I walked to our barracks. Pepi and Nekure and the rest of our team were still sitting around, drinking beer and talking. A few men had brought their senet sets and were playing. I cast around for any sight of my uncle, to see if he was watching me, as he'd threatened, but I couldn't see him.

"Do you fancy a game of senet?" asked Sabni as we neared our hut. "We could make one out of pebbles and sticks? I did that at home."

I shook my head. "No, thank you, Sabni," I said. "I thought I'd take a stroll, to make sure that I sleep well tonight."

Immediately, Sabni looked worried.

"You aren't going back to the tombs?" he asked.

"No, of course not!" I said firmly. "Not after what happened to me last time!"

"Can I go for a stroll with you?" asked Sabni. "It might help me sleep, as well."

"No," I said. "I need to be on my own."

His face fell when I said this. Inwardly, I groaned. The last thing I wanted was Sabni moaning to Pepi that he was unhappy because I'd gone off on my own. That would make Pepi suspicious and he might well come after me. And he'd be sure to come looking for me at the tombs.

I put my hand on Sabni's shoulder in a friendly way.

"I'm sorry, Sabni," I said. "I didn't mean to hurt your feelings. It's just that..." I hesitated, then blurted out, "I need to talk to my father."

"Your father?" asked Sabni, surprised.

"Yes," I said. "He died here." It was a lie, but Sabni wouldn't know that. And with Isesi and Huni no longer around, there was no one he could ask who would know the truth of where my father had died. I couldn't see him asking Uncle Minkaf. "I need to go to where he died and talk to his spirit."

"Is he buried here?" he asked.

That was a difficult question. If I lied and said "Yes", Sabni would be sure to ask where. But if I said "No", then Sabni would wonder how I could talk to my father without being beside his tomb.

"No," I said. "He's not buried here, but I know his spirit comes here, to where he died."

"How is that?" asked Sabni.

"I don't know," I admitted. "But I just know that when I go there, I feel his presence." Then I added hastily, "But don't tell anyone else. They would laugh at me and say I'm mad."

"I promise I won't," said Sabni.

"But we'll go for a walk tomorrow evening together," I promised him with a smile. "I know I'll feel better then."

Inwardly, I added to myself: tomorrow I will either feel better, or I will be a prisoner. Or dead.

Chapter twenty-two

I set off from our barracks, but in the opposite direction to the Mastaba tombs, just in case my uncle or one of his friends was watching me. My heart was pounding and it was all I could do to keep myself seeming calm.

I reached a corner where some of the streets from the area of the barracks went down an alleyway. I walked down the alleyway and past more streets, until I came at last to the edge of the barracks area. I was now a good distance away from the tombs. Anyone who was watching me wouldn't think I was heading in that direction.

Just to make sure, I sat down with my back against a boulder and looked up at the night sky, as if I was just taking in the night air.

I could hear the sounds of the desert at night: the dogs and jackals howling, the tethered donkeys braying as if calling to one another. As I sat there on the sand, with the enormous black sky filled with stars above me, I did something I hadn't done since I was really small. I began to talk to my father.

When my father had first died I had talked to him, or tried to talk to him. The priest had told me that his spirit lived on and that he would be watching over me. At the age of six I had tried to talk to him, asked him questions: why had he died and left me?

As I grew older and my life with my uncle and aunt grew harder, I tried talking to him again. I asked him why he didn't come back from the dead and save me from my uncle and aunt. But he never answered.

I guess I must have tried speaking to him a lot during those first years after he died, asking him what I should do, and for his help, but I never got an answer. Now, it struck me that maybe he hadn't been able to answer. He had been getting used to being in the Netherworld. Maybe since then he had wanted me to talk to him, but I hadn't.

At first, after he died, I had watched for signs that might show me he was watching out for me, but I had seen none. And so I had stopped watching. But tonight, I needed his help and advice more than ever.

"Father," I said. "I have been asked to help set a man free. This man says he is the rightful king of Egypt. He says if I free him he will make sure that no one suffers as they do at the moment. That the ordinary people like us will have a better life. That there will be an end to the misery of our lives.

"But Uncle Minkaf and Isesi and everyone else tells me that our life is the way it is because that is how the gods wish it. That nothing we do will change it. That this is the right way. But if that is so, why do the gods and goddesses treat us so badly and make our lives a misery? Why did you have to die, father? I know Uncle Minkaf says that because you died working for the King you will have a wonderful afterlife. But I want you here, with me! I wanted Isesi to be my friend now, not in the afterlife! I wanted to know my mother, and my baby brother as living people, not just in the afterlife! Why do all the good people die? What shall I do?"

Suddenly I found that I was crying, tears pouring down my face. I swallowed hard and bit back the tears in case they might bring someone else to me to ask what was wrong. Then I waited for my father's voice to come to me, to give me the answers.

But there was no sound apart from my own sobbing and the noises of the desert animals. There was no answer from anyone else to my question. The answer had to be my own.

Chapter twenty-three

I sat there for what must have been another hour. One side of me was waiting to make sure that whoever might be watching me got bored and went away. But another secret side of me sat and waited, hoping for an answer. Still none came.

Finally, I got up and looked around. No one seemed to have been watching me. But just in case they were, I hurried along one of the streets, then down an alleyway, then along another street and down another alleyway, zigzagging until I was at the other edge of the site and on the path that would take me to the tombs. It was late, but the site as I walked through it was still busy. Although most of the labourers had gone to bed, there was loud chatter and raucous singing from some of the men who stayed up late to drink and talk. The women who ground the grain were hard at work, getting the bread ready for breakfast in a few hours.

The smiths were also at work, making and repairing the copper chisels and saws that the masons used to cut and shape the stones. I could see the flames from their forges flaring brightly in the night sky, sending showers of red sparks flying as they hammered the red-hot copper into shape.

Now I had left the busy area behind and was on the path that led to the tombs, I took one last look behind me to make absolutely sure I hadn't been followed.

It was time. I had to reach the tombs while the lazy guards were on duty, before they changed over. I took a deep breath, and broke into a run.

I could feel my heart thumping the whole time I was heading towards the tombs. Finally I made it there. Large blocks of stone had been left lying around, ready to be hauled into position to erect the actual building that would cover the deep tombs. I reached the first of these blocks and hid myself behind it, scanning the area. There were no prisoners above ground tonight, enjoying the evening air. They were all down below in the tombs.

I scanned the area for the two guards, but couldn't see them at first. And then I did. As Ankhhaf had said, at least one of them was lying down, possibly asleep. The other was sitting next to him, leaning forward. For all I knew he might be asleep, too. But I couldn't take a chance that he definitely was.

I crept forward out of my hiding place, and crawled silently towards the next large block, my eyes on the two guards the whole time, waiting to see if they moved. Neither man did. The one lying on the ground stayed where he was. I thought I saw the one who was sitting next to him move a little and I stopped where I was and flattened myself against the ground; but he didn't move any more. Perhaps it had been a trick of the light and he hadn't moved at all, and my feeling of panic made me imagine it.

I waited for a while. Then, when I was sure neither guard was moving, I got up and crept forward again, as quietly as I could. I went from block to block, stopping at each block and waiting and watching and listening for any sign of movement from the guards; but none came.

Finally, I made it to the last block. Ahead of me was the opening to the shaft where I had seen the guards put Ankhhaf and the others down. And next to the shaft were the ladders, laid out on the ground.

I wondered if I would be able to move the ladder. Working as a labourer had made me strong, but these ladders were very long and made of thick wood. They would be heavy. It had taken two of the guards to carry one the previous time I was here.

I threw one last look towards the two guards. They still hadn't moved, but I was not going to take any chances I might be seen. On my hands and knees I crept out from behind the last block, and then crawled over the sand towards the ladders. I reached the ladders and took hold of the nearest one. I tried to lift it, but I could only manage to raise one end slightly, because it was so heavy. I would have to pull the ladder towards the shaft in the same way we pulled the sledges.

I crept along the length of the ladder until I was at the end nearest the shaft, then I took hold of it with both hands and pulled as hard as I could. The ladder shifted and slid along the sand. I worked my way backwards, hauling the heavy ladder along with me towards the shaft. All the time I kept shooting glances towards the guards, but I continued to be lucky. Finally I made it to the top of the shaft. I pushed the end of the ladder over the edge, and continued pushing it. The movement sent a shower of sand down the hole, and I heard voices from below. I recognized one of them as Ankhhaf. "It's the boy!" I heard him say.

I continued pushing the ladder over the edge, then the balance changed and the far end began to drop. I held on firmly to the top of the ladder to stop it falling and crashing down. The sound of voices from the tombs below was louder now, and I heard a sudden yell from where the guards were shouting, "What's going on? Who's there?"

The guards had woken up!

Frantically I ran for cover at the nearest block of stone, and made it just in time. The two guards were walking towards the shaft warily, holding their spears in front of them and looking about as if expecting to be attacked at any moment.

I hid in the shadow of the stone and held my breath, wondering what Ankhhaf was doing. Was he waiting to see what the guards would do? Was he even now climbing up the ladder, with his companions?

The two guards reached the area by the shaft and stood looking around at the desert night. Then one of them heard a noise from the shaft itself and he went over. He reached it and looked down, and as he did a figure leapt up from the shaft, grabbed him and tugged. The guard let out a shriek and toppled down out of view.

The other guard stood stock still, shocked, spear held motionless, as a man appeared from the edge of the shaft, followed by another, then another. It was Ankhhaf and his companions!

The guard suddenly came to life, but instead of rushing at the men as I thought he would, he turned and began to run away, yelling out, "Help! Escape!"

He didn't get far. One of the prisoners rushed after him and jumped on him, bringing him crashing to the ground. Then he leapt up, snatched up the guard's fallen spear, and thrust it into his body.

I was shocked. No one was supposed to die!

"Boy!" called the man with the spear. "Are you there?"

It was Ankhhaf.

I came out from my hiding place and went towards him. I looked at the dead guard on the ground next to him, and thought of the one who'd been pulled down into the shaft, and felt sick.

"You didn't have to kill him," I said, but even as I said it, it felt a very feeble thing to say.

"They would have killed us," snapped Mekhu, who appeared next to him.

"But you said ordinary people wouldn't die," I appealed to Ankhhaf.

Ankhhaf turned to me and, even in the night, I could see by the light of the moon that his face had changed. The honesty and kindness that were there before had gone. Now there was a different expression, one that looked more like a hungry jackal.

"Do not tell me what I said, mortal!" snapped Ankhhaf angrily at me. "I am your king!"

"He did help us get free," murmured Mekhu.

Ankhhaf looked intently at me, and for a moment I thought he was going to thrust the spear at me. Then he sneered dismissively.

"Very well," he said. "For the moment, he lives. He may even prove useful." Turning to his comrades, he ordered them, "Mekhu, let's get those ladders down the other shafts. We need to release as many as we can." He handed the spear to another of the prisoners and said, "Banefre, guard the boy. Make sure he doesn't raise an alarm."

With that, Ankhhaf and the other prisoners went to the ladders and began carrying them towards the other shafts where the other prisoners were kept.

"Right, boy. Stay there, where I can see you," said Banefre.

I didn't move. I was still shocked by what had happened, but especially by the change of expression that had come over Ankhhaf's face. The look of decency and kindness had gone, just like a mark in the sand blown away. In its place was the face of a dangerous animal.

"He called himself the King," I said, stunned.

Banefre shrugged and grinned.

"He tells everyone that," he said. "Ankhhaf likes to think he's royal. Maybe he is. Who knows?"

"You do!" I said angrily. "You knew him when he was a prince! When he was with the other princes at the royal court. You were his guards! You said so!"

Banefre grinned even more broadly.

"It was the only way we could think of to escape," he said. "Find someone who'd believe what Ankhhaf said and help him get out." He laughed. "If Ankhhaf had wanted us to pretend to be fish to get out of here, we'd have done that."

"So you were never guards at the royal palace?"

Banefre shook his head.

"No," he said. "Funny thing is, Ankhhaf believes we were. It was Mekhu's idea. Once we heard Ankhhaf start talking about how he was the true son of King Khufu, Mekhu told him he knew it was true because we'd been in his guard at the royal palace. Ankhhaf ate it up!"

"So Ankhhaf could be telling the truth," I insisted.

"Who cares?" shrugged Banefre. "All we wanted to do is get away from this place. Three years I've been here! Three hard, rotten, stinking years!"

"Ankhhaf said he was going to go to the palace and see Khafre," I said.

"And he might," nodded Banefre. "He's been here longer than we have. I think he really believes he's the true king. But he'll be going on his own. Once Mekhu gets back with the others, we're off. That's always been our plan. Free as many of the prisoners as possible. The more prisoners there are running loose, the better the odds that we'll get away from here." He chuckled. "It's lucky for you, your reward is to stay alive."

"And what is my reward to be?" asked a familiar voice from behind me.

I turned round and nearly collapsed with shock. Standing there, a club of wood in his hands, was my uncle.

"Uncle Minkaf!" I stammered.

Banefre stared at him, momentarily taken aback by his surprise appearance. Then he recovered and laughed.

"No reward for you, old man, except death," he said. With that he called out, and Ankhhaf appeared. There were about fifty prisoners with him. All had come from the tomb shafts where they had been imprisoned. I guessed that even now the ladders were being pushed down the other shafts for more prisoners to escape.

"So!" said Ankhhaf. "We have an intruder!"

"He's the boy's uncle," said Banefre.

"That's no reason for him to live," said Ankhhaf coldly,

and he took the spear from Banefre and pointed it at my uncle. "Time to die, old man."

"I don't think so," said my uncle calmly, and he held the wooden club in front of him.

Ankhhaf sneered.

"You think that piece of wood will save you?" he demanded sarcastically.

"No," said my uncle. "I think these men will save me."

He gave a call, and suddenly men came out from their hiding places behind the large blocks of stone.

Chapter twenty-four

There must have been over a hundred men, all of them armed with tools or clubs. None of them were men I recognized, they were all from other teams and gangs, men who'd worked with my uncle. At a shout from my uncle, the men rushed towards the escaped prisoners, lashing out with their weapons.

The prisoners were too shocked to respond. The prisoners were tough men, but their attackers were also strong – men used to their bodies taking physical punishment as a result of hauling tons of stones day after day. Many of the prisoners turned and fled immediately.

Ankhhaf launched himself at my uncle, fury on his face, lunging with the spear, but my uncle caught the point of the spear on his wooden club. I threw myself at Ankhhaf and jumped on his back, pulling back his head. As soon as I did this my uncle stepped forward and smashed his fist full into Ankhhaf's face. Ankhhaf dropped like a stone, taking me with him.

My uncle hauled me roughly to my feet.

"Well done, Nebka," he grunted.

There was no time for more words because the battle was continuing, but the imbalance of numbers soon bore out as the pyramid labourers battered the prisoners down, hitting them with clubs and lengths of wood, or smashing at them with chunks of rock.

Suddenly I heard more voices and shouts and realized that soldiers had arrived, armed with spears. But they arrived too late, the battle was already over. Some prisoners lay dead or wounded on the ground, while the rest of them knelt and cowered, their hands on their heads in a sign of surrender.

"What is going on here?" demanded an angry voice.

It was the Chief Overseer. He looked at my uncle and said, "Minkaf! Someone said you had brought these men here."

"I did," nodded my uncle. He put his hand on my shoulder. "My nephew, Nebka, overheard the prisoners plotting to escape and told me about it. So I told him to pretend to make friends with the prisoners and let me know when the escape was to be. He heard it was to be tonight. So I gathered some men that I knew so that we could stop it."

"Why did you not tell one of the overseers this?" demanded the Chief Overseer.

"Because the overseers have enough to worry about with the pyramid and the Sphinx to be built, as well as the pyramid and valley temples, especially with the arrival of our King Khafre on the site. If we had told one of the overseers it would have been his duty to report it to you, and you would have had to report it to the Vizier, who would have reported it to the King, and that might have disturbed the King and made him feel concern for the safety of the royal family. We knew we could deal with these scum without the King being troubled." He pointed at the prone figure of Ankhhaf on the ground. "This was the ringleader of the rebellion. With him rendered harmless, the rest won't be any trouble." He gestured at the shafts that led down to the tombs. "We've pulled up the ladders they put down, so the rest of them are quite secure."

The Chief Overseer barked an order, and the soldiers began poking the prisoners with their spears, forcing them to their feet.

"Get those ladders and put these scum back down where they belong!" shouted the Chief Overseer. As the soldiers carried out his orders, he turned to the pyramid workers and said, "You men have done well. You will all be rewarded for what you have done. But now, return to your beds. There is still a day's work to be done tomorrow."

My uncle clapped me on the shoulder.

"Come, Nebka," he said. "Let us walk back to the barracks together."

Chapter twenty-five

My uncle and I walked some distance behind the rest of the men as we headed back to the living quarters. I was silent, feeling more ashamed than I could say. I couldn't even raise my head.

Beside me, my uncle stayed silent, which somehow made it even worse. I was waiting for him to shout at me, hit me, rage at me for the stupid idiot that I knew I had been. But he said nothing. Finally, I said, "You lied to save me."

"Yes," nodded my uncle. "I could hardly tell the truth and have you executed. You are my brother's son, my nephew. You have been foolish and naïve, but you are not wicked."

"I didn't see you follow me," I said.

"No," said my uncle. "I was hiding behind the blocks near the tombs already, waiting for you."

"How did you know I would be going there tonight?"

"I didn't," admitted my uncle. "I hid myself there last night as well, just in case you arrived then."

I stared at him, stunned. Finally, I managed to ask him, "And the other men?"

"I have been coming here to work for many years," replied

my uncle. "I know lots of the men here. I guessed what might be going on, and spread the word among those I could trust who would help if this happened. A friend of mine hid with me last night and tonight. When I saw you, I sent him back to the barracks to bring the rest."

I hung my head.

"I have been stupid," I said. "I believed what that man told me."

"And what did he tell you?" asked my uncle.

So I told him. The things that Ankhhaf had said, about how he was actually the son of Khufu unfairly imprisoned; about how he wanted to bring fairness to all Egyptian people.

"But he didn't!" I burst out. "Once he was free he was as bad and as cruel as anyone! He killed the guards! He was going to kill you!"

My uncle gave a deep sigh, and put his hand on my shoulder.

"You have a lot to learn about people, Nebka," he said. "Many people will promise you things. Some of them will appear good and kind and honest. But not everyone is as they seem. Sometimes the apparently honest can be the worst sort of criminals, and sometimes those who seem brutal can be kind and gentle."

"Like you," I said.

My uncle chuckled.

"Sadly, no," he said. "I am what I am: I work the land."

He sighed. "I have not treated you well, Nebka. But I did that for a purpose. I know that life is hard, and I felt that you would need to be hard to survive it. So I have done what I can to make you hard." He sighed again. "Instead all I have done is make you hate me and despise everything I believe in. I have not been a good parent to you, Nebka. Your father would have done a much better job."

"My father may not have been able to save my life as you did tonight," I told him.

"Your father was a good man," said my uncle. "He would have given his life to save you. As it was, he gave his life so that you could have a better future."

"I know," I said. "But you have done a much harder job, Uncle. You have fed and given shelter to a miserable wretch who has been ungrateful and angry. And tonight you put your life at risk to save me." I shook my head in shame. "I am not worthy."

My uncle stopped and grabbed me by the shoulders and looked me firmly in the face.

"Don't ever say that!" he barked angrily at me. "You are worthy! You did what you did because you thought you were doing something good. Because you are young and naïve, you were duped. But you did it with a good heart. Unfortunately, men died here tonight because of your actions. But they might have died anyway. Those prisoners would have found someone else to help them sooner or later."

His fingers gripped my shoulders even harder, biting in deep. "Do you hear me, Nebka? You are worthy! If you weren't, I would not have bothered to save you!" With that, he released me.

"Now, enough of this. We need to get some sleep if we are to be able to work tomorrow."

And then he continued towards the barracks. I cast one last look back at the tombs, and I followed him. For the first time in many, many years, I felt I had a family again.

Epilogue
2484 BC

Many years have passed since that night at Giza. I am now a grown man of 45 with family of my own: my wife, Neith, and our two sons and a daughter, and a grandson. We work the land that once was my uncle's, where I was bought up. Uncle Minkaf and Aunt Ipwet are both long dead, but not a day passes that I don't give thanks to my uncle's memory, and trust the gods will look kindly on him in the Netherworld. He saved my life, and he saved me from my own foolishness. After that night in the quarries, I accepted his guidance, although there were still many times as I grew to manhood when he and I disagreed.

Ankhhaf was returned to work in the quarries, as was Mekhu and all the other prisoners who had been captured.

Was Ankhhaf the son of King Khufu? Or was he a liar? Although Mekhu and Banefre and the others may have lied, Ankhhaf seemed to believe in his own story. His attitude that night, when he announced "I am your king!" suggested so to me. Or was Ankhhaf simply so mad that he had led himself to believe his own story? I don't know. I do know that the next year when I went to Giza with my uncle, Ankhhaf was dead. They said he had been killed in an accident while quarrying. Huge rocks had fallen on him and crushed him to death.

I returned to Giza every time of the flood for the next fifteen years to continue the building work. From my third year there, I was chosen to work with my uncle on the team carving the Sphinx and building the Sphinx temple.

It was strange. I had hated and despised the Sphinx when my uncle had first shown it to me, but over the years I began to feel its power as I watched it develop, growing more like the painting every year. No, better than the painting, because this Sphinx was real. It seemed almost alive.

Ever since that first season at the pyramid site the same question comes back to me about the power of the gods. How is it decided who lives and who dies? How is it decided who will be poor and who will be rich? Who will be weak and who will be strong? And, despite all that our priests tell me about the gods and their divine knowledge, I do not know the answer.

By the time I became a father with children of my own, I was afraid for them. Would they live? Would they die? When would that happen? How? I didn't want to know. I just wanted to treat every day with them as it was: the most precious time of all. As my father had with me.

As I write this, it is the time of the flood again and my eldest son, Khaba, has gone to Giza. He is working on the pyramid for the new king, Menkaure, Khafre's son, who succeeded him when Khafre passed on to the Netherworld. Next year Khaba will take his son, my grandson, Djedefhor, to work with him. Djedefhor will be twelve years old, the same age as I was when I first went.

Khaba will show Djedefhor the great pyramid of Khafre, and the Sphinx, and tell him that I, his grandfather, built them. And when Djedefhor comes back he will want to know all about them, and I will tell him about my time at Giza, and what a great man his Great-Uncle Minkaf was. But I will never tell him about Ankhhaf and what really happened at the tombs that night. I have never told anyone, not my sons, not my wife. That was a secret between my uncle and me, and it will go with me to my grave.

Historical note

Although this book is fiction, it is based on evidence uncovered by archaeologists about life in the Old Kingdom of ancient Egypt: how the pyramids were built, the way of life for farmers, the food people ate, and so on.

The history of ancient Egypt is usually divided into different time periods:

PRE-DYNASTIC PERIOD, 8000 BC to 3000 BC: The drying out of the Sahara in about 8000 BC forced the population to move to the area along the Nile, where they farmed the fertile land. There were two separate civilizations along the river, one in Upper Egypt (the north), and one in Lower Egypt (the south).

EARLY DYNASTIC PERIOD, 3000 BC to 2686 BC: The two civilizations of Upper and Lower Egypt unite. The time of the first Egyptian kings and queens. There is debate as to who was the first actual king: Menes or Narmer, or perhaps they were the same person.

OLD KINGDOM, 2686 BC to 2160 BC: Time of major developments in Egyptian sciences and engineering, including pyramid building.

First Intermediate Period, 2160 BC to 2055 BC: A time of famine and civil war.
Middle Kingdom, 2055 BC to 1650 BC: Lower and Upper Egypt reunified. Expansion of Egypt's empire.
Second Intermediate Period, 1650 BC to 1550 BC: Civil unrest due to weak pharaohs.
New Kingdom, 1550 BC to 1069 BC: Increase in Egypt's power, and a growth in learning and skills (such as the world's first glass-making and the first known maps).
Third Intermediate and Late Periods, 1069 BC to 332 BC: A time of civil war between rival kings, as well as invasion by Nubians, Assyrians and Persians.
Ptolemaic Period, 332 BC to 30 BC. The time from the rule of Alexander the Great to the death of Cleopatra.
Roman Period, 30 BC to AD 395: Egypt becomes part of the Roman Empire.

The River Nile

The Nile is the world's longest river. It is 6,650 km long, and runs from central Africa north through the entire length of Egypt.

The Egyptians were aware that their very lives depended on the Nile, and they viewed it as a sacred river, the giver of all life. Not only did the annual flood of the river fertilize the growing lands on either side of it, but in the far south of Egypt the waterfalls and rapids of the Nile were a major obstacle to any invading armies. Egyptians used the Nile to transport people (including soldiers), livestock, foodstuffs, quarried stone, and much else besides. It was the main artery of communication for the entire country and Egypt's major trade route into the Mediterranean.

Egyptian religion

The ancient Egyptians believed that life was controlled by gods. If the gods were offended they might take revenge on the people on Egypt.

The first of the Egyptian gods, and the most important, was the sun god, Ra. All pharaohs claimed to be descended from Ra, which made them gods. (In medieval England, kings also claimed to be descended from God, which gave them a Divine Right to rule).

Ra was believed to be the god who brought fertility to the soil of Egypt by making sure the Nile flooded each year. The Egyptians feared that if Ra was insulted by the people of Egypt, he could stop the Nile from flooding and cause famine. The Egyptians believed that every evening the sun god, Ra, was swallowed by the sky goddess, Nut; but every morning Ra was reborn.

Other gods and goddesses included:

AMUN-RE: the next most important lord of the gods after Ra.

OSIRIS: the son of Nut and Geb (Nut's sister). After being

murdered by his brother, Seth, he became ruler of the Netherworld.

Isis: Wife and sister of Osiris.

Horus: Son of Osiris and Isis. The falcon-headed god.

Seth: The god of Chaos.

Anubis: The god of the Dead. The jackal-headed god.

The pyramids and the Afterlife

The pyramids of ancient Egypt were built as tombs for the god-kings, the pharaohs. The first pyramid was built for King Djoser at Saqqara by Djoser's architect, Imhotep, around 2650 BC. Djoser's pyramid is known as the Step Pyramid because it has six levels, each with a flat surface at the top, like massive steps going up each side.

The first pyramid in the recognizable pyramid shape, with flat sides, was that of Sneferu, who ruled from 2613–2589 BC. His pyramid is noticeable because the four sides bend inwards as they near the peak, giving it the name "The Bent Pyramid".

The Great Pyramid at Giza was built by Sneferu's son, Khufu, and it is this pyramid that established the structure and shape we are familiar with today.

Inside, many pyramids were filled with stone rubble and even mud brick. Deep inside were passageways leading to the burial chamber in which the sarcophagus of the dead king was placed. Often, false passages and empty chambers were built to fool possible grave-robbers.

Once the king had been laid to rest in the burial chamber, the passage to the chamber was sealed with large blocks of granite.

The last workers to leave the interior of the pyramid after the burial did so by using an escape passageway. This passage was then closed with stones that were identical to all the others used in the construction of the pyramid so that no one would be able to find the way in. Because of this, the entrances to the pyramids remained secret for thousands of years after they were built.

The pyramid complex did not just consist of the main tomb: it also included two temples to maintain the spirit of the god-king after death in the Netherworld. Nearby smaller pyramids were also built as tombs for the queens. To the ancient Egyptians death was not an end to, but part of the journey of life.

The key to this was the *ka* and the *ba*, which together, they believed, made up part of the soul or spirit of the person. It was believed that when a person died the *ka* and the *ba* went to rest in the Netherworld and joined a whole mass of other spirits. There they waited while the physical body was mummified and laid to rest. When that was done, the *ka* returned to the mummified body to live in the afterlife. This is why so many artefacts have been found in pyramids. Not just food and jewellery made of gold, silver and precious stones, but also statues, musical instruments, clothing, cosmetics and furniture. In the case of King Khufu a magnificent boat was found sealed in a pit by the pyramid for him to sail in. All of these artefacts were there to ensure that the god-king had as good a life after death, in the afterlife, which was a *parallel* world, as he did during his time on Earth.

The *ba*, however, now journeyed on and could travel anywhere in this world. This became the roaming spirit of the god-king and could be conjured by priests, or those making offerings to the cult of the pharaoh. Meanwhile, the royal aspect of the spirit of the dead god-king was absorbed by the next king, who continued the royal line.

It is worth pointing out that during the Old Kingdom this transfer of power applied to kings and not ordinary people. This can be seen by the doorways at the sides of the pyramids. Only kings and priests could enter through these doors; commoners were barred.

Technology in ancient Egypt

Ancient Egypt was at the forefront of developing technology, thousands of years ahead of Europe. Mathematics and geometry were crucial to the building of the pyramids.

Papyrus for writing on (made from beaten and pressed strips of the papyrus plant) were produced in Egypt as early as 2850 BC and much later sold to the ancient civilizations of Greece and Rome. The blades of the chisels and saws used for cutting and shaping the stones for the pyramids were made of copper.

Despite their advancements in technology, the ancient Egyptians did not use the wheel until invaders brought it with them in the sixth century BC. It has been suggested that they did not use the wheel because they had no need of it; their existing technologies were sufficient for their needs.

Mummification

Mummification of the dead body as a way of preserving it was only for the rich. The poor were buried in shallow graves in the sand. Because of the extremely dry environment, this often resulted in the bodies of the poor being mummified naturally.

When the rich and powerful, such as kings, were mummified, the first step was removing all the internal organs of the body that could putrefy: including the stomach, liver, intestines and lungs. The heart was left inside the body because the ancient Egyptians believed this was where the essence of a person was to be found.

The internal organs were then dried in a salt-like mixture and placed in jars, known as canopic jars, which would be buried with the person. The brain, however, was discarded.

The body, now mainly skin, muscles and skeleton, was placed in natron, which was a kind of salt, for forty days. This mixture dehydrated the body to preserve it. The body was then wrapped in layer after layer of linen bandages, sealed to the body by resin or a tar-like substance called bitumen.

The whole process took about seventy days from the time of death. Only then was the body ready to be buried.

The Sphinx

For years arguments raged amongst archaeologists about when the Sphinx was carved. Many put it as being built at the same time as Khafre's pyramid. Others claimed it was built much earlier, possibly in the time of Khafre's father, Khufu. Those archaeologists claim that weathering and erosion of the Sphinx, especially erosion by water, showed that it was actually built before 3100 BC. However, other archaeologists produced their own evidence to show, in their view, that when other factors such as acid rain, thermal expansion and the poor quality of some of the limestone used on the building of the Sphinx, it seems it was more likely to have been carved during Khafre's reign. The most exhaustive and recent evidence in Mark Lehner's book *The Complete Pyramids* (republished by Thames and Hudson in 2008) supports this theory, which is why I have opted for it being carved during the time of Khafre.

Senet

Senet is believed to be the oldest board game in the world and was invented in ancient Egypt about 3500 BC. It is a bit like a cross between chess and ludo, with white and black playing pieces. Senet is still made, and played, today.

Acknowledgements

With thanks to Dr Kathryn Piquette, formerly of the Institute of Archaeology, University College London, for her many helpful comments, about the text of *Pyramid of Secrets*. Any historical inaccuracies that remain are my own.

My Royal Story

Vividly imagined accounts of queens and princesses from the past.

Turn the page for an exclusive extract from

My Royal Story: Egyptian Princess

Prologue

Egypt circa 1490 BC

Perhaps Senenmut's right. Maybe sometimes I *am* just a stupid, headstrong little girl. I'll admit it, I scared myself badly yesterday. What if I'd broken a leg making that jump, rather than just spraining an ankle? Hulking great soldiers in my father's palace guard have died from as much. One week a "crusher of nations" the next a corpse on the embalmer's slab. There's not much you can do to mend a broken leg. In our climate, infection sets in fast.

It's an uncomfortable thought. I don't want to die. Not yet. At thirteen summers old, I've hardly started.

But then what none of the men in the court of my father, King Thutmose, remotely understand is how boring life can be in the harem. Even dear Senenmut, my tutor. They think all women are the same. They think we just love to sit around each and every day, feeling protected, while *they* strut around looking powerful, having "important conversations". Well not me. I watch some of those girls, plucking their lovely eyebrows, smoothing their shapely legs, rubbing lily-scented ointment into their perfect skin, and wonder what's going on inside their heads. Answer – not a lot! Lamps lit but no one at home, I reckon.

Me on the other hand – I like *doing*. The more active I am, the better my brain works. When I've been running, I just feel so alive. "Don't you ever get tired?" the girls ask. Or (with a faint look of disgust) "How can you stand getting so sweaty?" Or that old favourite (me doing press-ups by the garden pool), "You'll never get a man if you keep doing that, Asha! No one wants a woman with muscles!" I was probably about six when I first heard that one. Well, actually no, I don't get tired. I have *more* energy after a run. Great big wonderful ideas spiral around me. I can feel my *ka* leaping and bouncing for joy. In that moment I think I was born to change the world. I can even pretend I understand Senenmut's arithmetic classes. And I *like* the feeling of sweat trickling down my back, the tingling in my body when I drive myself to the limits of speed and endurance. Any man who wants me will just have to love me for who I am. "*I promise before Amun I will cherish thee, Runner Girl…*" Runner Girl! It's what the other girls call me. As nicknames go, it's not the worst, is it?

But yes, I'll have to think more carefully from now on. *Obviously* roof-running is dangerous – that's partly why I like it – but maybe I've become overconfident. Nofret, daughter of Mutnofret, may be my best friend as well as my half-sister, but I hadn't listened to her. When we'd walked the course the previous day, she'd spotted what I was choosing to ignore.

"Are you *really* sure about that jump, Asha? Looks a bit of a stretch to me."

I'd been peeved she'd questioned my judgement. "No problem!" I'd answered, brushing her away, "I can take *that* any day. Watch me go!"

So yesterday at dusk, we'd sauntered past the guards to our chosen starting point, the highest roof of the harem, three storeys up, by the Queen's Tower. It was a perfect evening. A magnificent blood-red sun was sinking behind the cliffs of the western desert. On the far side of the River Nile, the narrow valleys where the royal ancestors rest were deep-cut black scars against the pink ribs of rock. In the nearer distance delicate billows of grey-white mist drifted up slowly from the sacred river as fishermen, washerwomen, boatmen and traders all desperately tried to cram two hours' work into the last hour before sunset. Around us, beyond the harem and the vast palace complex, sprawled the countless grey mud-brick houses which make up the great city of Thebes, capital of the Two Kingdoms of Egypt, the place where every Egyptian dreams of living. This, *all this* and so much more, is the world he rules: the great Pharaoh, son of the sun god Re, Thutmose, peace and prosperity be on him for ever. My dad.

"Have you ever thought," said Nofret, "how strange it all is?"

"What do you mean?"

"We could have been born anywhere. You or I could have been a slave girl. Or a peasant woman, grinding corn all day. Not the daughters of a king."

And for a moment we paused to take in that extraordinary piece of good fortune.

The very end of the afternoon is the best time of day for roof-running, while there's still just enough good light, before Thebes' citizens come up to eat, talk and hold hands in the night air away from the heat and stink which builds up down below among the houses. As I unwound the linen shawls from my upper body, swapping the long sheath of my day dress for a running skirt, the gentlest of breezes began to waft across the rooftops from the north. It brought with it the faint aromas of baking bread and cooking food.

"Ready then?" I said, stretching and twisting. (Here's a tip for you. *Always warm up before you exercise!*) Nofret nodded. She's such a loyal companion, my older sister. We may have different mothers, and we don't look anything like each other (me lanky and plain, she small and pretty), but we think like twins. She doesn't want to run, she's always made that quite clear, but she's never once mocked my favourite pastime. And she's never hinted slyly to anyone that I'll "grow out of it in time". That's a line she leaves to my mother, Ahmose, the King's Great Wife, chief woman of the harem.

"Don't lose count, will you?" I added. As if.

"Just take care of yourself, Asha," she said. "You worry about the jumps. Let me worry about the counting. On your marks … get set … go!"

And I was away, bounding down over the harem roofs. The first hundred paces would be the last hundred paces of my return. Then I curved away down towards the harem gatehouse, leaping over it and out into the suburbs by way of the shops outside the gate, still way above ground level. The smell of bread was at its strongest just there, the odour fading in my nostrils as I leapt from the roof of the last shop on to the houses beyond.

Why should I do such a daft thing? Well, haven't you ever looked at the birds of the air and wished you could be like them? Roof-running's the closest you can get. When I'm up there, I'm free and fully alive, every sense finely tuned, a thrill running through the whole length of my body. But don't *you* go trying it, not unless you have the kind of protection the goddess Hathor and the mother of the gods Nut give me.

Of course, part of the fun's doing something I'm not supposed to. There's no rule that says I shouldn't be outside the harem on my own – the guards aren't there to keep us in, more to keep unwanted people out – but yes, I understand full well people could think it's *unseemly* for a princess, even a thirteen-year-old princess, to jump around the way I do. Especially without telling someone in authority where I'm going and what I'm doing. But what harm is there in it? Let's be honest, to any ordinary Theban I meet while I'm sky-skimming, I'm simply another anonymous, annoying street kid. I'm away and gone far too quickly for them to guess who I am.

Over the houses, I was running parallel to a dirty, manure-filled street. How can people live in such filth? At least up on the roofs there are no animals to trip over, and so, unlike down at street level, there's no dung to leave my legs splattered and smelly. The narrow passageway below me meandered left and right for maybe 200 paces. I twisted and turned with it, leaping the short gaps between the houses every fifteen strides or so. Occasionally a face peered inquisitively at me from a stairwell, and I shot them a reassuring friendly smile. No, I wasn't there to steal their family heirlooms!

At the end of the houses were some stables. I comfortably made the longish jump across the space just there, pulling myself over a parapet wall, legs and bottom slithering and flailing over the mud-brick. No marks for style, but an interesting view for anyone down below! On the far side was another similar wall. I vaulted it fluently and began the flat-out run to the jump Nofret had worried about. The blood was pumping now. In that moment I believed anything and everything was possible. Silly Asha! Overconfidence is such a dangerous thing. I drove my legs full tilt at the leap across the chasm, not giving a thought to the drop, but as I pushed off into mid-air the mud-brick underneath my leading foot crumbled. In that instant, knowing I'd misjudged the jump badly, that Nofret had been right and I'd been wrong, perhaps for the first time in my life I felt fear. Truthfully, the thought of serious injury or death had never occurred to me until then. Now for a terrifying split-second I thought I was going to crash to the paved yard beneath and break my neck. In despair I lunged for the edge of the roof, and the goddess Hathor, praise her name, must have been watching over me because as I fell my stretching hands miraculously found a hold. My feet scrabbled at the mud-brick wall, my whole body jolted and shuddered, but somehow I clung on, and then slowly, painfully, was able to haul myself up on to the roof, safe and more or less in one piece.

I sat there for a while collecting myself, shaking from the shock, looking dumbly at my bruised and bleeding knees. I could just imagine the tutting of the harem girls. "*Oh, look at silly little Asha! When will that girl ever grow up?*" Feeling a complete idiot was bad enough, but then the agony in my ankle kicked in, and I realized what carelessness can cost.

When I tried to stand, my right leg wouldn't bear any weight at all. I clung to a wall for support, and waited miserably for Nofret, knowing I'd have to eat humble pie when she eventually found me.

Which she did, of course. She knew roughly how long the run should have taken – a count of about a thousand was what we'd guessed. When I didn't arrive she fluttered her eyelashes at Senbi the nice young harem guard to come and help her look for me. He didn't need much encouragement to spend a little time close to pretty Princess Nofret!

"Oh, you poor thing," she said, when they finally spotted me leaning against a chimney, trying my hardest to be a brave Pharaoh's daughter and not cry, "You gave me a real fright. I thought someone might have kidnapped you. Whatever would I have said to Father if a ransom note had arrived at the harem?" Leaning on their shoulders, I hopped home feeling very small and stupid.

Enlisting Senbi's help was good and bad. I couldn't have staggered back without him. But questions were quickly asked about why he wasn't where he should have been and then he had to confess to his boss that, sorry, sir, he'd been AWOL rescuing the Princess Hatshepsut, and then Senbi's boss blabbed to my tutor, Senenmut, and so this morning there I was explaining myself to a committee comprising my mum, a stern-looking Senenmut and Inet, my nurse, equally severe. It wasn't a happy interview.

So there you have it. I'm gated, watching the harem girls on their hopeless quest for ultimate beauty until my ankle heals. But as I said, running makes Big Ideas happen. And trust me, after yesterday, I've got a really good one brewing.

Because of course my Big Idea is … yes … you've got it … the papyrus you're holding in your hand now. Treat it very, very carefully! There's been nothing like it, not in the 1,500 years since the great warrior and first Pharaoh Narmer joined up the two kingdoms of Egypt. True, the walls of the temples are covered in writing and our libraries are full of miles and miles of fading documents. But most of that boring stuff was scrawled by old men desperate to leave something behind before they died and made their final journey out to the stars. Believe me, nowhere is there a story like the one I'm going to write. A true story. An exciting story. Well, it's bound to be. It will, after all, be the tale of a Pharaoh's daughter. Look after it well, whoever you are. Maybe it will bring you luck! Maybe my *ka* will live again through you.

So, to begin at the very beginning, let me tell you exactly who I am.

My name's Asha – you know that already. But the common people of Egypt know me by my official royal name – Hatshepsut, only daughter of King Thutmose by Ahmose his Chief Wife, Queen of Egypt. My name means "First among noble women", and maybe one day I *will* be truly noble. But inside my head and to those who love me best, I prefer to be simply Asha.

Soon the star Sirius will rise in the sky, which means that tomorrow the five days' celebration of the New Year begins. As my New Year token, I promise that from now on I'll write down truthfully whatever happens to me during the coming months and years – the good *and* the bad – the time in which my mother Ahmose keeps assuring me her daughter will stop being a silly girl and magically turn into an accomplished, mature woman. As if, by gaining a few feminine curves, she thinks I'll lose my "inclination to foolishness" (i.e. the roof-running!) and become sweet, obedient and interested in weaving. Dream on, Mum. Pigs might fly!

Senenmut smiles indulgently on me and encourages me to write – it's his job – but if my father were ever to find these ramblings, he'd probably tell me to burn them at once. And no doubt Shushu the vizier, the man I call "the vulture", the man closest to the King's ear, would agree with him. Which is exactly what I'd expect of such an unpleasant man. "Women are all very well. In their place!" I've heard him say more than once. Which doesn't stop his liking for vain, glossy harem girls. Especially Esho. I've seen the way they look at each other. Ugh!

But I'll outwit Shushu and the others who want to keep women under their thumb. Doesn't *my* story deserve to be heard as much as any man's? Since in Egypt women can buy land and have a house built, or trade jewellery and corn, shouldn't their lives and opinions matter as much as men's? Go on, let's think the unthinkable. Couldn't a woman one day even become Pharaoh and rule as wisely as any male? Would it so disturb the great god Amun and the *maat* of Egypt?

Maybe that's a word which means nothing to you. *Maat*. It's what our royal family and court exist for. To protect Egypt, and by everything we do to achieve harmony and well-being for our people. It's a sacred duty. And a pain in the neck. We royals may have wonderful palaces in which to live, the best food and clothes, all we could ever want, but we live daily in the knowledge that if we get it wrong and anger Amun, he may punish us and all Egypt with us. And it would be our fault. *My* fault! Imagine carrying *that* responsibility around with you every day.

When I've finished a year's scribbling, my papyri can conveniently disappear into some safe hole in the ground. Then perhaps when I'm an old woman, I'll go and dig them out, and amuse myself reading about me when I was thirteen, before burying them again for you. But first things first. How am I going to manage tomorrow, hobbling up to the temple of Amun for the New Year festival? I'll have to get there somehow, even if Nofret and Senbi carry me. It's something I wouldn't miss for the world.

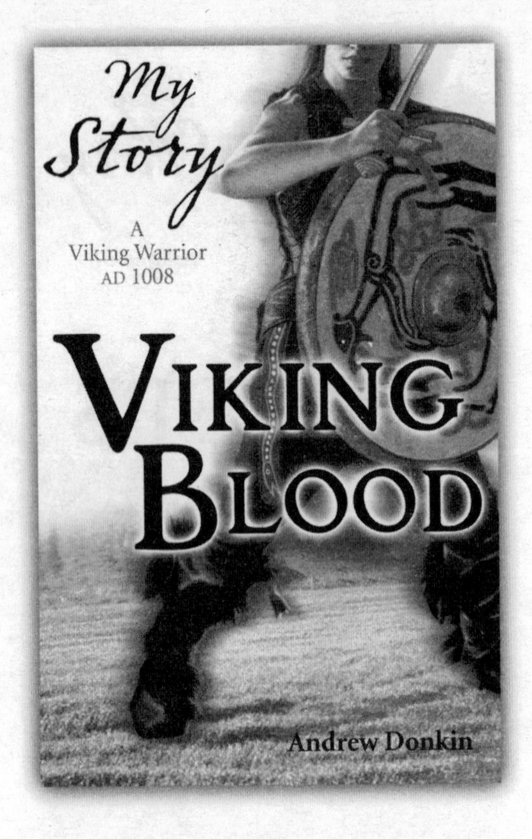

It's AD 1008, and after being injured in a raid that goes horribly wrong, Tor Scaldbane is devastated at losing his chance to be a legendary warrior.

But then he discovers the sagas of his ancestors: glorious, bloody battles, ancient heroes, powerful gods ... and realizes that all might not be lost after all...

My Story

A
Second World War
Spitfire Pilot
1939–1941

BATTLE OF BRITAIN

Chris Priestley

It's 1939 and Harry Woods is a Spitfire pilot in the RAF. When his friend Lenny loses his leg in a dogfight with the Luftwaffe, Harry is determined to fight on. That is, until his plane is hit and he finds himself tumbling through the air high above the English Channel...

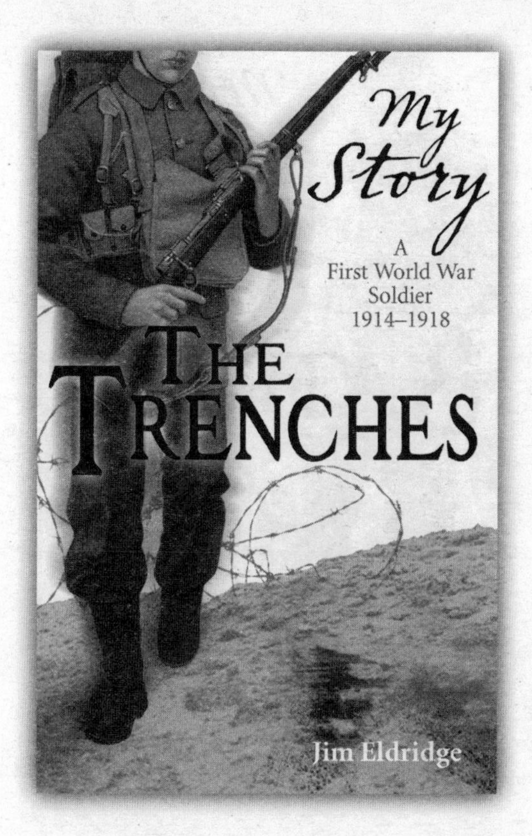

It's 1917 and Billy Stevens is a telegraph operator stationed near Ypres. The Great War has been raging for three years when Billy finds himself taking part in the deadly Big Push forward. But he is shocked to discover that the bullets of his fellow soldiers aren't just aimed at the enemy...

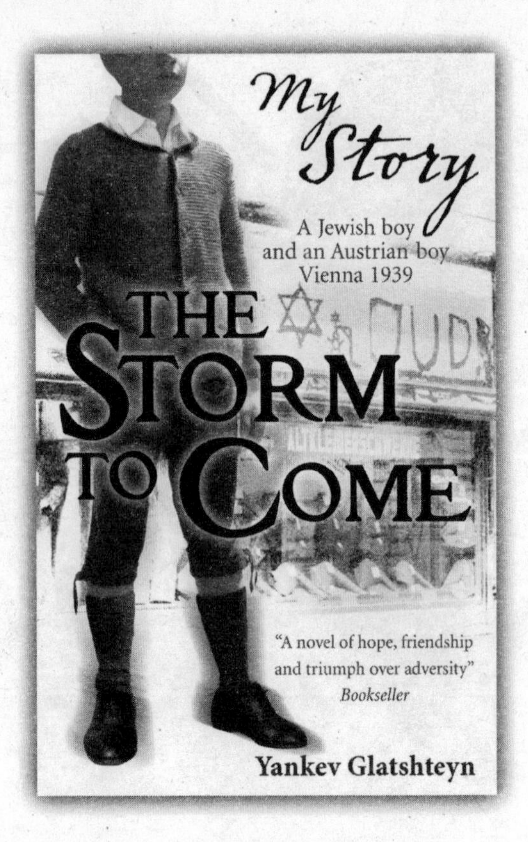

Emil and Karl are best friends. Emil is a Jew; Karl isn't. When three men take Karl's mother away, who knows where, and the Nazis murder Emil's father, the two boys find themselves alone and scared, wandering in an increasingly hostile city. Who can they trust and where can they go...?